East Is West of Here

Books by Joyce Thompson

35¢ Thrills
The Blue Chair
Hothouse
Merry-Go-Round
Conscience Place

EAST IS WEST OF HERE

New & Selected  Short Stories

Joyce Thompson

BREITENBUSH BOOKS
Portland, Oregon

First Paper Printing August, 1988
2 3 4 5 6 7 8 9

Library of Congress Cataloging in Publication Data
Thompson, Joyce.
    East Is West of here.
    I. Title.
PS3570.H6414E37   1987   813'.54   85-5689
ISBN (cloth) 0-923576-32-x
        (paper) 0-932576-58-3

Breitenbush Books acknowledges the support of the National Endowment for the Arts, a federal agency, for a grant which helped to make the publication of this book possible. The press also wishes to express appreciation to the membership of Northwest Writers, Inc. for their support.

Breitenbush Books are published for James Anderson by Breitenbush Publications; Patrick Ames, Editor-in-Chief. General Editorial Offices: P.O. Box 02137, Portland, Oregon 97202.

Distributed by Taylor Publishing Company
            1550 W. Mockingbird Lane
            Dallas, Texas 75235

Manufactured in the USA

The author gives special thanks to Rosellen Brown, for her example, as well as for her generous introduction; to the many friends who have inspired and sustained her; to the National Endowment for the Arts, for helping to fund this publication; and to her children, Alexandra and Ian, just because.

The author and publisher give their thanks to the National Endowment for the Arts, a Federal Agency, for a grant which aided in the publication of this book.

Grateful acknowledgment is given to the publishers of the following publications for permission to reprint stories that first appeared in:

Ms. Magazine, Colorado State Review, Writers Forum, Dark Horse, Mississippi Mud, Tuesday Night;

Fine Lines: The Best of Ms. Fiction (Scribner's, 1981);

Thirty-Five Cent Thrills (Lynx House Press, Amherst, MA, 1978)

Contents

Introduction

A long time ago, having been dragooned into editing an issue of a (now defunct) literary journal, I had one of those editor's rewards that happen just often enough to keep us doing our duty like bemused rats tapping for a pellet, opening those Manila envelopes, scrawling those kind rejection slips: I found a genuine story, a "real thing" piece of writing that joyously announced the presence of impressive talent and the skill to turn sheer charm into a structured accomplishment.

I had come upon Joyce Thompson's "The Afternoon of a Poetess" and I was so impressed that I sought out its author (who turned out to be newer at the game than I'd dared imagine) and we've been friends ever since— or, as writers on opposite coasts have to do it, pen pals.

Joyce Thompson has expanded marvelously as a writer in the intervening years, author of novels and screenplays as well as stories, creating for her characters some of the more imaginative and unusual situations in today's fiction. From her first novel, *The Blue Chair,* to her most recent, *Conscience Place,* she has shown herself to be good at something all too unusual: she has managed to combine real characterization, poignant and subtle, with "speculative"— some would say science fiction— intricacies of plot. Her inventiveness seems boundless; so does her sympathy for the "real" people caught in its toils.

But what she does in her stories is more classic, more modest, yet no less profound for its modesty. It is intriguing to see how she has pursued through many years and many changes, through extremely varied situations, a preoccupation already evident in "The Afternoon of the Poetess." The eleven-year-old, who has her own designs on the glamorous life of a poetess, pictures herself "far from my present self...I live now," she says, wise already in the promises and the snares of the imagination, "for the person I will become." Already she can see how fulfilling it is to dream; at the same time, she understands (redesigning her body while she's about it) how unsatisfying life-in-the-future can make life-in-the-present.

It is the obsession of these stories that we are never wholly at home in our moment; that we are always, or at least often, time travelers of the psyche, willing ourselves ahead into sweet un-precedented satisfactions or—more frequently, given the dis-astrous history of love and need—dreaming ourselves backward so that we can try our lives again, like a melody, from the top. Again and again Joyce Thompson's wistful protagonists undo the fabric of present life so that they can knit it up again in a dif-ferent, a more beautiful, design. All the wasted possibilities, the impossible choices, the traps, the "almost was" and "could have been," the "didn't have to be so" and "never will be again," and, not least, the "here I am forever," come to rest, delicately poised, in her stories, heartbreakingly familiar, plausible, irreversible.

Her characters—lovers, mothers, widows, rejected husbands, political radicals—have the intelligence to realize what they have lost or will never have and they mourn but rarely pity themselves about it. (That, of course, is what's so welcome about the *short-ness* of stories: we are in the situation and out again before the characters can turn tedious and begin to belabor their pain.) Only the little girl who knows she will be a poetess, for whom it is not too late (and who is already a performer, an unselfconscious story-teller far funnier and more insightful than she can imagine) will actually inhabit the self she dreams about. The others are barred by reality, by the irremediable permanence of fact, from living the alternatives that haunt them.

Joyce Thompson's stories possess all the grace and wisdom an optimistic editor dared dream for her those many years ago on that afternoon of her own making.

Rosellen Brown, Houston, Texas

To my father,
who likes to get right to the point,
and to my mother,
who savors all the charming eccentricities
along the way,
this book is dedicated,
with love.

Ice Flowers

BEING WARNED that a madman will howl under your windows when the moon is full does not prepare you for it when it happens. Nothing can prepare you for it— that first night when the strange voice penetrates your dreams and you mistake it, at first, for some nightmare voice of your own. You shift under the covers, burrow deep, trying to protect yourself against this renegade inside you, until at last you wake and see the moonlight, and know it is not you.

You get up, finally, and go to the window that lets the moon-light in, because no matter what is there, not to see it is worse than seeing it.

It takes you awhile to find him, hidden in the tree trunks and almost as slender. When you do see him, it is as shape only, a negative exposure on the dark woods that close around your house. His hair is silver, long and wild. It is the realest thing about him. You look for the moon that does this to a man. As you find it, a dark cloud bites down on it and leaves a jagged scar.

He is not talking to you now. He talks to the trees, and to the horses. They have stolen out of the woods and gathered at the paddock fence to listen— three dark shapes and one white, tails twitching nervously, hooves pawing the dark earth.

His voice drops now and he speaks to them privately. Is he talking horse? Horse breath makes clouds in the night. When they turn and gallop off, dismissed, they leave a vapor trail behind them. He speaks again, and now you are sure he is speaking to you.

Being warned that a madman will howl under your window when the full moon comes does not prepare you for the fact that he speaks brilliant nonsense that cuts into your heart.

He turns to go now, and you return to bed. When he reaches the kennel, the dogs explode; their barking shatters the calm. When you get in bed again, your husband stirs enough to reach out a hand to find your thigh and ask, "What is it?"

Once they've started, the dogs do not stop barking easily or all at once. They excite each other, spur each other on. "What scared the dogs?" your husband asks.

"It was him," you whisper. "It was Mr. Hart."

Your husband's name is Tom. His work is a drug that puts him to sleep, exhausted, and a goad that drives him early from your bed. In the morning, you tell him about the visitation. It did not penetrate the pillow he put over his head, did not seep into his dreams. Only the racket of the dogs aroused him; that is the kind of music he, a veterinarian, is wired for. "Next time," he tells you, "wake me up."

You query the neighbors. Hart is older than you guessed, past sixty. Italy. Fast cars. Fast women. Madness. No one knows more. Fourteen years in an asylum, then release. For seven years he has been the nearest neighbor of your house, and you have

2

lived in the house one month, while one moon shrank and grew.

As long as you live here and he lives there, the visits will not stop.

He is not seen by day, though he walks the woods with his dogs and knows, knows everything that happens in your house and in the neighbors'.

He never washes. He is covered with boils.

His dogs have mange.

There is nothing you can do.

He is a well-connected madman. When his people bought him his house, they bought the local police chief, too. Complaints will go unheeded.

Is he ever lucid? you ask them.

No one knows.

It is the first of many visits. Some nights your husband wakes up, too, and mourns his broken sleep. His body and the demands he makes of it are in a race, and there is no slack in his schedule for the howling of madmen. One night he jumps from the bed, wraps himself in his bathrobe, goes to the window and throws it open. The cold rushes in. You get up, too.

"Hart! Mr. Hart!"

And the face, always hidden before, raises up, reveals itself, wreathed by the wild, white hair.

"Oh, Dr. Tanner. Good evening, sir."

It is not much of a revelation; the eyes continue in hiding, two stars shining at the bottom of two deep wells.

"Why don't you go home and go to bed?" your husband says. "It's three in the morning."

"I would if I could, but she..." he gestures at the moon, "will not permit it. I have business to transact, with these trees, with these beasts."

"Can't you do it during the day? I need my sleep."

"I never sleep. I seem to have lost the hang of it. And it's so comforting, to do one's business in the dark."

"Well, you have no business here." Your husband's voice is tense, and you put your hand, a hand intending caution and restraint, on his arm.

"Please," you whisper gently, "please don't."

"And my wife. You frighten my wife, coming around like this."

"My respects to your wife. Is she there with you now, young Mrs. Doctor?"

Your flesh prickles. He knows you from the trees.

"She is. And she'd like to go back to bed, if you'd give us some peace and quiet."

"A thousand apologies. I don't wish to disturb you. But you see, I act under compulsion, almost exclusively, when the sky is in such configurations. I intend you no harm. Please tell your wife I wish her good rest, and pleasant dreams."

"Jesus Christ," your husband says. The words freeze visibly. He slams the window shut. "Does he always have to sound like he's playing Hamlet, for Christ's sake?"

"Mrs. Winter says he went to Oxford."

"Good," your husband says. "Fantastic."

You go to bed, and go to sleep in silence.

It affects everything somehow. That voice. The voice slides between you and your husband, pushes you, ever so slightly at first, apart. He comes home to you later and less passionate, speaks less and less. It is not your fault a madman howls under your window at night, but both of you begin to believe that it is.

You have plenty of time alone, to contemplate the voice and what it means. Sometimes it speaks pure poetry. One night

Hart finds a book you've left on the dashboard of the car and asks to borrow it. Next morning, it is gone, and every night for a week you leave a note in the same place the book was:

Dear Mr. Hart:

I hope you enjoy *One Hundred Years of Solitude.* When you finish, won't you come by some evening and discuss it? Early evening. Your postmidnight visitations disturb my husband; he needs his sleep.

The note remains, untouched, until it fades. Two weeks later, the book appears one morning on your welcome mat, wrapped in a rag to keep it dry in the finely sifting snow. No note of thanks, no word at all.

Then, suddenly, the visits stop. Your husband relaxes a little and is less fierce, but his nascent scowl remains. The voice is his pain, and he knows too much about pain to put faith in remissions.

You miss the voice. You hope that Hart is well.

All through February, the days are crisp and brilliant. It only snows at night, and the predawn freeze makes every new snow snap and squeal under your boots. Winds litter the whiteness with the elegant black brushstrokes of fallen twigs, and it is good to be abroad, making your way through the woods with your dog and both of you half-crazy with the excitement of the cold. You follow him, the dog, to the edges of the river and what he shows you there— ice grafted onto nature in sculptured elegance— arrests you utterly.

Ice flowers. Ice grass. Ice twigs. Ice stones. Clear and pure as crystal things, though it is a long time since there was any glass-maker with skill like this. When you have looked your fill and risen, you see the tracks behind you in the snow—one set of human feet and several dogs. You put your own foot in the clearest print to make sure it isn't yours. It is a longer, thinner foot than yours, Hart's foot. If he came once, he may again. You wait. Throwing sticks for the dog is your excuse for waiting, and you stay out until four o'clock nightfall forces you to think of home.

Your house is empty except for its warmth. You are only beginning to thaw when the telephone rings and you pick it up expecting to hear your husband say he won't be home for dinner yet again.

Instead there is a long silence. You speak into it, self-conscious. Who? What? At last, just as you are about to hang up, "Mrs. Doctor Tanner, are you there?"

It is a moment before you know it is *the* voice, it is so shrunken and altered by the apparatus through which it reaches you.

"This is Charles Madison Hart."

You can hear the breaths between his words, always lost before in the night air, and hearing them seems intimate and makes him real.

"I wanted to explain why I can't come to call, and why you shouldn't ask me. I appreciate your kindness very much, you know."

"Then come. Please come at a reasonable hour and come inside and have a cup of tea."

"I can think of nothing more delightful. But I must decline."

"Why?"

"Because of what I've done."

"What have you done?"

His pause is pure flirtation. Then, "I've done quite terrible things. My sister could tell you, except she's too discreet. You know my sister?"

"I scarcely know her."

"Then take my word. And my regrets. I'm quite mad, you know. The doctors couldn't cure me, so they let me go."

"You sound fine now."

"I am. I am. But it's nothing one can count on." You hear him sigh. "As it is, I'm an unpredictable fellow, unfit for any but the life I live. Dangerous, that's what I am. And why I can't accept your kind invitation."

"It stands," you tell him. "If you change your mind."

"My mind changes itself," he replies, before the line goes dead.

In March, you come under siege. His visits become a persistent nightmare and peace an occasional exception. Your husband is wire tightly coiled away from you. The nightly visitations subtract sex from his schedule and you become a lame duck bedmate, a neutered teddy bear, soft, warm, and sexless. Your skin is hungry and your nerves go into mourning. You begin to dream about the dead.

Outside your window, a madman plays King Lear or makes up his own poetry for trees and shingles. Some nights he too dreams sex and shouts his fantasies— perverse, inventive, terrible fantasies— at your barren window. His lust shines in the night. It is a lust of the mind that remembers bodies, distortions nostalgic for reality. Your own dreams twist and turn upon themselves, have you mating with women and trees, never far from the edge of an ice-choked river just melting into spring, and you wake up ashamed.

One night a strange thing happens. The voice is there, the message is lust, and just as the image grows orgasmic, your husband groans in his sleep and instead of falling back deeper into pit and pillows, raises up and rolls on top of you and takes you, not tenderly, but hard and fast, with unaccustomed passion. He says nothing and you answer with a silence of your own, but you are pleased, relieved, encouraged. In the morning, he doesn't remember.

But morning is his time of power, when he solves problems and his energy, renewed by sleep, seems endless. It is morning, then, when he appears unexpectedly and pounds the table with an emphatic fist.

"We've got him," your husband says. "We've finally got him."

"Got who?"

"Got Hart." His grin shows teeth. "I filed a complaint about his mangy dogs, running loose. They're awful things. Nearly bald, half of them, and going mad from the itch." Your husband's eyes zero in on yours. "He's either got to kill them or cure them." He pulls a paper from his shirt pocket and unfolds it. "I estimate that to cure them, it'll cost in the neighborhood of fifteen hundred dollars. Isolation for a month, and treatment. Plus food. It adds up."

"What if he doesn't want them cured?"

He lays an imaginary shotgun against his cheek, squints down the barrel and pulls the trigger. "Then pow!"

"Why, Tom?" you ask. "He's harmless."

"He bugs the crap out of me. I haven't had a good night's sleep in weeks. And it's criminal to let animals run around in that condition. It's cruel." His lips lose their fullness and become a grim, straight line set in his jaw.

It does not silence Hart. Instead his visits start earlier, just past midnight, and go on longer, sometimes almost till dawn. They are pleas now, not performances, and have a single theme.

"Don't take my dogs away. You mustn't take my dogs away."

Your husband gets less sleep than ever, but now takes a kind of malicious pleasure in his forced insomnia. He smiles at the ceiling, night after night, awake and listening.

The pleading tears at you. "For God's sake, Tom, go talk to him. Tell his you won't hurt his dogs. Tell him they'll feel better without the mange." So you plead, too, and he refuses to answer either one of you, just stares at the ceiling, arms crossed behind his head. "Please, Tom. Maybe he'll go away if you'll only re-assure him."

"If he wants to talk, he can come to my office or call me on the phone. Otherwise, forget it. He doesn't exist."

The man who doesn't exist continues to cry out under your windows, and finally, you can't stand it anymore and sit upright and start to swing your legs around. "Then I will."

"No!" His arm swings out so suddenly and hard that when it hits, it takes your breath away. You fall back flat on the bed. He offers no solace or apology. You turn away from him and cry.

The voice goes on. "I beg of you, Doctor Tanner. Don't take my dogs away."

They take the dogs by force. The dog catcher's van is accompanied by two state troopers and a public health officer in a sleek police car. When he sees he is outmanned, Hart flees. The dogs scatter, in the woods, along the river, through the golden stalks and stubble in the fields. The men give chase.

Just picture it, the five of them, running fast as they can, encumbered as they are by ropes and nets, by guns and big men's boots. They trample the fields; they sweat and swear; they tear their pants on broken branches. As they close in on one dog on the river bank, about to snare him, one of the troopers steps back incautiously and plunges half his leg into the river's molten ice. He screams. They start at two in the afternoon. By five they have captured all but one, one wily dog, who still outsmarts them. Five dogs taken. Five dogs cower in the catcher's van.

"Maybe we should come back tomorrow for the other one," the public health man, out of breath, suggests, but four pairs of eyes glare back at him, four panting men refuse as one. Hell, no. For this is a religious war.

They stand watch near the entrance to the woods. The sun is at a low slant on the fields and the evening chill makes it seem winter is coming back. All but defeated, they stand. One damn dog, one mangy dog outstanding. Their curses steam. *And then.*

And then, they see a small form dash across the field and take cover behind a golden stand of stalks.

"It might have been a rabbit," the public health man says.

"That was a *dawg.*"

"How the hell we gonna catch a dog at this distance? He'll be in the woods before we cross the road."

"Like this," the wet-legged trooper says. His sock is slowly freezing around his calf. He plants the butt of his rifle on one beefy shoulder, lines up the stalks, and chambers a round. They wait in silence till the small form moves.

The trooper fires. Fires again for good measure. Five prisoners, one casualty. They call it a good day's work.

Your husband tells you all about it, with manly glee, and you listen because you have no choice, but after dinner you go to the bathroom and retch up all you've heard and eaten. Going to bed that night, you are equally afraid of your husband and of what the voice will say. It does not come. Your husband sleeps.

Next morning, when he's gone, the telephone rings.

"Your husband is a cruel man."

You can neither agree nor disagree, for different reasons.

"You should leave him."

You tell Hart what you tell yourself. "He's my husband. I

married him."

"I want to see my dogs. When can I visit them?"

"You'll have to talk to him. To my husband."

"I wouldn't like to do that. Tell him, please."

"I'll try, but ..."

"No"

Hart takes a smart revenge. Every night he sits outside your husband's clinic door, saying nothing, quite circumspect in behavior but so strange and awful in his appearance, with his ragged clothes, his boils, his matted hair, that he scares your husband's clients and makes small children cry. The dogs bark incessantly, his own dogs loudest of all. He will not speak to you; your husband will not speak to him. The wholly-owned police chief will not make him move away.

The dogs are cured. Your husband, perhaps not feeling his victory is complete, will not release them to Hart, but calls his sister, Mrs. Welton, to come and claim them.

"My, don't they look nice and healthy. Thank you so much, doctor," she says, and writes a check for fifteen hundred and twelve dollars right then and there.

And you wouldn't have known unless, years later, in another incarnation, with another husband at your side, you quite improbably met up with Mrs. Welton at a cocktail party, and she told you: that when you left, her brother Charles went to your husband's house and beat on the door relentlessly until he opened it, then seized Tom by the shirt, shook him hard against the door frame, eyes ablaze, and asked and asked again: *What have you done with her?*

You tell Mrs. Welton to thank her brother for his concern, to tell him you have prospered in another life.

11

The Stud

"I HAVE lots of aunts," Brian observes, as we amble hand in hand up the beach which, because of mist and the bluster of sea wind, we have entirely to ourselves today. "But you're my only uncle."

My response is a carefully noncommittal "hmmm," pitched just slightly higher than the "hmmm" of the ocean.

"Marta says," Brian continues, "that you're the only good man she knows."

"Hmmm."

"Except me."

Now he lets go of my hand and abandons the perilous topic, too, having spotted the parliament of seagulls gathered thirty yards beyond us on the shore. Nearly a hundred birds strut and peck in a ragged but cohesive circle, closely packed and gray enough that when I squint, it seems to be the sand itself that's moving. Brian races headlong toward them and the congregation explodes like a shell, scattering bird/shot in a dense pattern against the white mist sky.

13

Marta is Brian's mother. He is my son. The offended gulls hover, scolding him; the bravest or most cynical of them are already landing again on the sand. Brian's red jacket is the only color on the beach. I can hear his thin delighted laugh, his pleasure in disruption as I walk slowly, steadily toward him.

Marta is neither my wife, nor my lover, is barely my friend. Actually, she was a cohort of my ex-wife in the days before the Women's Movement made a battleground of our marriage, where all the advantage of indignation was on her side. I protested to Sandra, my estranged spouse, that it wasn't and never had been me preventing her "self-actualization," stopping her short of a Ph.D., making her stay home to feather our empty nest. I'd be thrilled, I told her, if she wanted to go back to school or get a job or run for Congress. It was her independence, I averred, her ambition, that attracted me to her in the first place.

Sandra was in no mood to buy my avowals of innocence in the matter of what she perceived to be her stunted growth and oppressed condition. Never mind that I did half the cleaning, much of the cooking, and all the laundry. The piece needed a villain, and I got the part, not for a handlebar moustache or a black heart, but because of the extroverted urogenital equipment between my legs, a particularly crude form of typecasting. Our union gave way before a flood of grievances, not before Sandra, in a righteous spirit of vengeance, managed to divest me of a good portion of my earthly possessions, as penance for the harm she did herself and attributed to me. Marta, as a member of the consciousness-raising group which I still hold responsible for precipitating the decline of our marriage, was present in court for the divorce as a show of support for her "sister."

The sisterhood was mostly fictional; in both the days before she accepted the Movement's mandate to love all fellow human beings possessed of vaginas and days after she outgrew it, Sandra

14

found little to like, much less love in Marta, calling her in the first case an aggressive bitch, and in the latter, with the jargon mastered, a lunatic separatist radical. Sandra, after several years of playing out the arrested adolescent rebellion for which I served as the authoritarian object to be pushed against, returned her craft to a steady course, not much different from the one she pursued before the storm. Marta, though, continued as a kind of pirate ship on the high seas of liberation.

Liberation meant to Marta, among other things, the freedom to be fat. Even in the days when she was counting calories in order to conform to the ideal of beauty legislated by the male oppressor, Marta was, let us say, *zoftig*. Now, feminist, she is simply enormous, her own ideal of beauty being, apparently, the Venus of Villendorf, whom she comes, with the addition of blue jeans and large heptagonal blue plastic glasses, more and more to resemble.

Brian, by contrast, is not fat at all. Amid the reassembling congress of gulls, he seems almost birdlike himself in his red jacket, slender, anyway, a little forlorn? My bony genes will out, despite his mother's carbohydrate ministrations. His metabolism, like mine, is swift. His hair, like hers, is almost black and very curly, his skin Greek olive, without the patina of oil Marta's exudes. He hails me, and the lifting of his arms startles the flightier gulls into a quick ascent.

"Do seagulls live in families?" he asks as I approach.

"This certainly looks like a clan gathering."

"I mean real families," Brian says. "You know, a father and mother and kids."

"Kids are baby goats, Brian. I don't know what they call baby gulls."

He punches my arm. "Don't be silly. Do they?"

"We could look it up."

15

"I think," I tell him, "that the concept of the nuclear family is unknown to seagull culture."

"What's a nuclear family?"

"It glows in the dark and explodes when dropped from high altitudes," I tell him, at the same time ruffling his rough curls. If he were my son, I find myself thinking, his hair would be close-cropped, but he is my son in fact only, not by right, and Marta prefers him cherubic, his maleness disguised and softened.

"I wish I lived in a real family," Brian says, pressing his slim self closer to me as we walk.

"Come on. Let's run up those dunes and slide down." I grab his hand and pull him along at a gait that makes conversation impossible. We scale the dunes with giant strides, our shoes filling up with sand, and then descend. I take a flying leap for momentum and Brian follows my lead. At the foot of the dunes, sandy and panting, Brian climbs on my chest and I hug him tightly. He is only five years old.

"Want to do it again?" I ask him.

"Want to marry Marta and be my dad?" he asks.

I press him closer for a moment, then struggle to my feet and toss him, kicking and giggling, over my shoulder, carry him all the way home.

Brian is asleep in bed. Marta wholly fills, almost obliterates my old nubbly green armchair from view, her swarthy face ashine in the firelight, and I find myself trying to remember if she was this big, this monumental, when Brian was conceived. She reads avidly, Erica Jong's latest, trying to catch the tarnished idol out in heresy. From the way her pen busies itself with marginalia, I gather that lapses of doctrine must abound. When she pauses to look into the fire, I pose my question. "Does Brian know who his father is?"

"Of course not."

"What have you told him? He must have asked."

"I told him," Marta says, in her deep though oddly nasal voice, "that his father died before he was born."

I never asked before and the news now makes me shiver despite my sweater and the glowing alder flinging sparks across the hearth. Marta's eyes drop to the book spread open on the expansive convexity of her stomach. She considers the subject closed.

I don't. "He wants us to get married so I can be his father. He proposed to me today."

Marta laughs, and it is laughable, I suppose. I have no more desire to marry her than she does to be my or any other man's wife. Still, something important is at stake. I want my son. The words form so clearly, so forcefully in my mind that for a moment I think I must have spoken them, but no. Marta's expression is almost amiable, still amused, as it would not be if I'd advanced my claim of paternity aloud. She watches me, waiting to be released to return to her reading. "I was looking for a sire, not a mate," she says.

The words (she's said them before, in the present tense) bring back the time: Marta seeking me out, appearing unexpectedly about a year after Sandra and I parted company. I'd moved from one state to another, to a remote coastal town, so she had to have spent some effort tracking me down.

"I'm going to have a child," she announced.

I congratulated her. "Who's the father?"

"You are," she said.

I was quite sure I was no such thing. She saw the disavowal on my face. "I'm not pregnant yet," she amended. "But I want to be. I came to ask you to do the honors."

"Why me?"

She ticked off the reasons on her fingers. "You're highly intelligent." That was one. "You appear to be physically sound." She
looked up. "You are, aren't you? No diabetes, no hemophilia?"

"No," I said. "I used to have migraines, but I seem to have out-
grown them."

"You're not bad looking," she continued, "and you're non-
aggressive. I don't know if that's a genetic trait or not, but I'm not
taking any chances. Finally, I trust you to be discreet."

"I'm not sure I understand."

She laughed then, delivering the line. "I'm looking for a sire,
not a mate. I'd offer to pay you for your services, but I imagine
you'd be offended, so I ask as a favor."

Amid the chorus of objections I could hear my ego, basso,
crow, and I began to understand the willingness of certain Nobel
laureates to ejaculate in test tubes. Sandra, though a fine vessel,
was never eager to bear my child. "I'd have a hard time contrib-
uting support," I protested. "I'm barely supporting myself these
days."

"What I want," Marta said, "is to raise a child myself. No
support necessary. No strings."

"You want me for my sperm."

"That's right," Marta said.

"He'll get over it," Marta says. "This father thing. He only wants
one because his friends have them."

"It's a pretty basic human desire," I point out.

"Nonsense. Brian has all the love that any child could want.
I'm parent enough."

In terms of size, this is surely true; Marta makes two, perhaps
three of me. "Do you play ball with him? Do you fix his bike?
How about hiking? Do you take him hiking?"

From behind the enormous glasses, she regards me with de-

18

tached amusement. "Do you want to marry me?" she says.

"No."

"Well, then. . ."

One week a year, they come to visit me, Marta's old friend, the only good man she knows. I have seen my son five times. This annual visit was my one condition in agreeing, finally, to Marta's unconventional request. Why I made it I have never been sure; at the time, I convinced myself it was in the spirit of scientific inquiry, to requite a natural curiosity and nothing more. Marta readily agreed. She likes my home, my coastal town, my cooking, my willingness to spend every waking hour with Brian while she reads or sleeps. I am a good babysitter. A good man.

"Don't you ever feel swamped? Unsupported?" I ask Marta, the sprawling mother goddess in my chair. "Don't you ever wish you had some help?"

"I do have help. The Single Mother's Cooperative is excellent. Brian has an infinite number of aunts."

"So he told me. And I'm his only uncle."

"I don't seek out the company of men."

"What about role models? Aren't you afraid you'll turn him into a little fag?"

Marta lifts one massive shoulder in a shrug. "What's wrong with that? I like homosexuals better than most men. At least they're sensitive."

"That's a stereotype."

"By reason of the truth behind it." Marta's yawn makes a hole in her doughnut-round face. "It's not your worry," she tells me. "I'm going to bed."

Nightmares wake Brian and he seeks comfort in my bed. I make a nest for him in the covers, am careful not to touch or disturb him, but sleepily he rolls toward me, a small warm animal burrowing. I am tremulous with father joy, and scarcely know how to sleep myself, with this trusting child asleep beside me.

In the morning I am scolded for taking him in. "Pandering to his weakness," Marta calls it. "You've probably undone months of work." She seems truly angry and I wonder if it's not because he came to me, not her.

Sun today, and I push Brian in the tire swing I've made him in the ancient madrona tree in my yard. Marta, a lover of darkness, naps with her book, while her son, mine, flies through the autumn morning air, startling birds from the upper branches with his shrieks.

"Did you know my father?" Brian calls over his shoulder. "Before he died?"

I am stunned by the question.

"Did you?"

"Yes."

"Was he big?" Brian asks me. "Was he brave?"

Even as I consider it, I recognize the futility of a custody suit. The stud regrets his service. Marta is a vigilant mother. For five years, she's had her way.

"Uh, how do you know you'll get pregnant?" I asked her.

"I've been plotting my cycle. This is the peak of fertility."

Even though my mind finally acquiesced, my body had reservations. Marta lay below me in requested darkness, unmoving. It was useless to explain the need for stimulation, the concept of pleasure. For her it was a clinical procedure, a necessary evil, with no enjoyment sought or to be given. It was not to Marta I made love, but to an elaborately conjured fantasy of Liv Ullman.

Scenes from a Marriage was on TV that month.

When I turned on the light, after, Marta had already pulled the sheet up to her chin. She was smiling. "It happened," she said.

"How do you know?"

"I felt it. I know."

We showered, separately.

I dream of killing Marta, but my waking self, a pacifist, disowns the dream.

"What did he do for a living?" Brian asks. "Was he short or tall? Were you friends? Was he smart? Marta will never tell me anything about him," Brian says. "Do I look like him?"

"You look something like him," I say.

By candlelight we eat my lasagna, a deceptively familial triangle at the wooden kitchen table.

"I wish this week would last forever," Brian says.

Marta tells him to finish chewing before he talks.

"I've been thinking," I tell Marta, late on the last night of their visit. "You know, I'd be happy to have Brian stay with me summers. It would give you some time for yourself."

"I have plenty of time to myself," she says.

"I'd like to have him."

"We agreed to a week."

The fire has burned low. By its light, Marta is shiny red and shadow, a gross sculptural exaggeration of the female form.

"I could tell him the truth," I threaten. The truth, I've decided, is my only weapon.

I see her teeth in the firelight. "If you do that, you'll never see him again. We made a bargain."

"I love him," I say, but she only smiles.

Their bags are in the car. Brian clings to me. Marta shakes the car keys in her hand. "Come on, Brian. I have to be at work tomorrow. We've stayed too long already. I'll have to drive like the devil to make it back on time."

The words hover on my lips, a secret message for my son, but Marta wrests him from me and deposits him in the front seat of her Datsun, slams shut the door. "We'll see you next year. Brian, put your seat belt on."

He cries to leave me. I hold back my own tears until the car turns left, begins its southward migration at the corner of my street.

No, Brian, I answer at last. Your father was not brave.

The Christmas Party

YOU ARE the daughter of a special man— that first of all— in a land where people dress in movie costumes, clothes that are long and flowing and eloquent, nothing like the Sears Girls Department ruffles you wear, or the blue-with-a-whisper-of-red-stripe suits your father wears, or your mother's black cocktail dress and rhinestones, rhinestones better than diamonds because they're so big and bright they proclaim themselves phonies right up front, no pretense (think about that one— later it will come to mean Art above Riches, and you will live by it), and you really are able to learn/think/know all these things at once. The thoughts don't come in words but wash around you like deep currents in an intimate warm ocean and that's why you can think so many things at the same time, and in this land, girls can be the heirs apparent of their fathers *and* honored for their own achievements. Here being female is no disability—

"You gonna jump or not?"

The boy hangs one-handed from the bunk bed ladder, directing his sneer upward at the girl perched one hand on the ceiling, two feet on the guard rail of the top bunk.

"Jump. Are you afraid or what?"

The girl stares at two six-shooters on the wallpaper. One is aimed, one holstered. A belt floats near them, no cowboy inside.

"Jump."

The girl does not want to jump. She has stood here too long, thinking about jumping. For a moment she makes herself imagine what will happen if she doesn't jump, and then casts off. It is a fast fall from guns past cowboy boots and snaky lariat to the cactus near the floor. She lands badly, on her wrist, and has to keep her face averted to hide a surge of tears. The boys don't applaud, that would be too much to ask, but at least she has won their silence. Behind her, Jerry thumps down. The floor vibrates under cropped brown carpet. Thump. Thump. Howard and Davy land.

"It's your turn, Melissa," Jerry says.

Over her shoulder she calls back, "You go ahead." She can hear Jerry climbing. Thump. Davy whoops, falling. Thump. The girl turns and leans against the cactus on the wall. The boys climb and jump, climb and jump, faster and more daring because she watches them.

And in this land, being young is not a strike against you, and neither, for good measure, is being old, and all this is important because you feel sorry for your grandmother, so proudly poor, and are impatient to be recognized for the effulgent being you know you are, and in this land it is possible to be pretty and perky as a Mouseketeer and smart and deep besides. It is a land of few limits and no rules.

Beige-blonde poufs materialize around the doorframe, frivolous around the sharp-eyed face they halo. Jerry's mother's

24

mouth is lipsticked hard, bright red and her earrings flash the small, discreet sparkle of real emeralds. Her voice is boot camp stern. "You children quiet down now. Even in the living room it sounds like World War Three in here."

Eyes on the carpet, the boys cluster around a common guilty smirk. Jerry's mother glances at the girl. "At least Melissa knows how to behave like a lady."

The girl concludes that Jerry's mother must be stupid, not to understand how quickly her praise will turn to poison.

"Find something quiet to play," Jerry's mother says. "And don't leave Melissa out."

"Don't leave Melissa out," Davy echoes, as soon as Jerry's mother leaves. "She's such a little lady." His head minces side to side and he talks through his nose. Malice or mucus curdle the words.

The girl knows better than to talk back. It is less fun to tease her if she doesn't respond. They will not make her cry. This is a promise to herself. She will not cry.

"Wanna play Monopoly?" Jerry says.

Davy says, "Melissa's too little."

"I know how to play Monopoly," the girl says. She would be happy to play a game with rules.

"Naw," Howard says. "It's boring."

"So what do you want to do?"

Davy shrugs, loose-shouldered. Howard says, "I have to go to the bathroom."

"Let's all go," Davy says. "Except Melissa. She can't come."

The girl does not want to come. For as long as the boys are gone, she can relax. When their foot thuds subside, she can hear the rustle of the grown-up party in the living room, a low flat murmur peaked by laughing. Most of her parents' friends do not have children; usually, she is allowed to make herself invisible among the adults and watch them. Sometimes one of the childless women will take a fancy to her and pay attention. The attention feels so good it makes her face glow. This exile among the sons of her father's colleagues feels like damnation. The girl wraps the ruffles of her Christmas skirt tight around her knees and stares at the notched pine timbers of the bunk bed.

In this land boys are neither cruel nor stupid, their faces do not stretch into crude monster shapes between babyhood and adolescence but retain their delicacy. Boys are kind and wise and do not dedicate themselves to villainy. Everyone knows that courage is more than how high you will jump down from, and intelligence is more than bragging, and you are very special here. In this land, your father is proud to call you his apprentice. He teaches you the secrets of medicine, and while he heals with his hands, coaxing or shoving damaged bones back into their proper configurations, you heal by intuition, and your father is impressed by your gift.

The boys explode into the room. Laughing and chewing, they sputter crumbs. Jerry holds out a yuletide cocktail napkin balled around a broken Christmas cookie. "Here, Melissa."

The girl is more grateful for the prop than for the sweet. She chews slowly.

"We snuck into the kitchen," Howard says. "We watched the grown-ups."

"They're getting drunk," Davy says.

"Your father's drunkest," Howard says. "He fell into the Christmas tree."

"It would have gone clear over," Davy says, "except Jerry's mother caught it."

"Jerry's dad caught him," Howard says.

"You should have been there, Melissa," Davy says. "It was the funniest thing I've ever seen."

26

The boys mime the action. Howard staggers into Davy's arms. Their laughter shrills. The cookie has dissolved around walnut shards and the girl rolls nuts on her tongue. She does not know what drunk is, exactly, but she knows that it is bad, not something doctors are supposed to be. "You're lying," she says.

"Are not," Davy singsongs. "Are not lying."

Jerry looks at the girl with what might be kindness. "My dad is kind of drunk," he says. "He keeps singing Christmas carols."

Swaying, Howard warbles, "Jingle balls, jingle balls, wiggle all the way." The girl blushes while the boys howl. Davy grabs the girl's arm and pulls her toward the door. "Come on," he says. "Come see for yourself."

"I don't want to," the girl says, but Davy tugs at her arm and she knows it's another dare, something she has to do no matter how much she doesn't want to. She slaps Davy's hand away. "All right. Let's go."

At the door, the boys rise up on tiptoe, slouch like spies. "Shhh," Davy cautions.

The girl hesitates. "We'll get in trouble. Your mother said to stay in your room."

"They'll never catch us," Howard says. "They've forgotten all about us."

This is a chilling thought, more so because the girl suspects it's true. Somehow being present in her parents' minds keeps her alive. If they are capable of forgetting her existence, there is every possibility she does not exist. Something cold and liquid shoots up the empty space beside her spine. She leans against the wall, under grouped photographs of Jerry's relatives, and tries to retreat to that special land where there is no pain, but the path she travels there, that shining synapse, is somehow jammed and she is stuck in the hall, in the inexorable present. Unable to escape, she follows the boys.

Heads stacked like the grimace-faces of a totem pole, they crack the kitchen door. The girl's heart seems to have dissolved into a fluid pulse that beats everywhere inside her, hair roots to toes. At first the grown-up party swirls like an oil slick, a giddy mix of sounds and colors, until she steadies her senses by the Christmas star on top of the tree. Thick and furry as a caterpillar, her father's voice worms its way into her ears. "Give me my car keys, you son of a bitch, or I'll deck you."

Her eyes follow his voice to his body and arrive in time to see her father, propped against the entry arch, plant his palm hard and flat against Jerry's father's chest. Jerry's father rocks backward, then rights himself. Beside the men, her mother is unmoving, stiff as her Christmas curls, eyes bright and bitter as the rhinestone grapes cascading down one velvet shoulder.

Davy's whisper is triumphant. "You see?"

In this land, you have no parents. You are strong and brave and everyone expects great things of you. You are never sad to have no father and no mother, because in this land, orphans are thought to be special, children of the whole tribe, of the world.

The sidewalk is an icy channel narrowed by mounds of snow. The girl steps carefully in her slick party shoes. Half a block ahead, arms locked under his armpits, Jerry's father and Howard's father half-guide, half-carry hers. Her mother totters behind them on treacherously thin, steep heels. When the three men slip and crash down into a hard pile on the ice, the girl stops walking and lifts her face to the sky, lets her eyes graze among the winter constellations.

You are seven years old and cannot hear their curses for the wind.

Robert's Song

I WAS driving my daughter to kindergarten when I heard the song. The radio was tuned louder than befits my age to the rockabilly station that seems, these days, the best compromise between nostalgic muzak re-recordings of '60s rock and simplistic S & M outcries of my juniors. Not, she protests, that I grudge the current inhabitants of youth's blessed ghetto their musical expression, only that I say, with due respect, it is not mine. I too turned seventeen in '65; I run with Jackson Browne on empty.

But the point is that I heard the song.

Braked at a stoplight, I told my five-year-old, "Mommy's old friend wrote that song."

She was interested, not so much because of my acquaintance with the composer as by the idea that songs are written at all. A good deal of magic still operates in her world; things happen there without human agency, they simply are, have always been. Radio is, when you think about it, a grand abstraction. Maybe she believed until that moment that a song comes into being as it is sung, or that my hand on the on-knob was the musical prime mover. She listened attentively as I accelerated and sang along.

"Is that your friend singing now?" she asked me.

It wasn't. Robert's voice was a lyrical tenor that he could squeeze into an angry, anguished falsetto that used to sound to me as I imagined the race collectively must feel about the no-win proposition of being human. The voice coming out of the radio was husky by contrast, and far too cheerful.

"Which friend?" my daughter asked me, and began to list all of my friends she knows about, with the curl of an imaginary question mark at the end of each name. I joined the ritual, and to each name told her no. Finally, when her litany of names was exhausted, I said, "It was my old friend Robert," and she responded, as she always does to history lessons, "When I was really little." It's no use trying to convince my child that the world or I existed before she did. She rejects the concept of 'before you were born' in favor of an imagined time, roughly the length of all eternity, when she was present but not conscious, a time experienced but lost to memory, and I have stopped trying to persuade her otherwise. Some of my own mother's stories are so vivid I can see and feel and smell their settings; I know the flowers were yellow roses, although she's never told me so. So with my child. I accept her participation in my past.

Who's to say she wasn't there the night Robert wrote that song, the night his guilt-enlarged prostrate kept him crouched all night on the toilet in my apartment, with his twelve-string guitar laid across his bony bare knees? In the other room— the living and bed and dining and thinking and dreaming room, twelve feet by twelve— I pretended to but couldn't sleep. The bathroom door stood slightly open and a long thin slice of light slid out to touch my mattress on the floor. I listened.

Robert's process of creation sounded to be a sort of wrestling match against an unseen enemy, or maybe several, each trying to defeat him in a different way. A few bars of melody would sing out from his guitar, followed by a strum of frustration, all dissonance. His voice would rise high and clear in lyric pronouncement, then dissolve into curses and mutterings. Sometimes he tested words in a rhythmic monotone, a kind of idiot's chant repeated over and over, that deprived them of all sense, until suddenly they came out joined to a musical phrase that elevated them into meaning once again. Sometimes he argued, heatedly and elaborately, as if there were something there besides the washstand and the bathtub to argue back. Sometimes too I heard a trickle of urine and his grunted protests at the pain of urination. The toilet flushed.

Around dawn, just as darkness began to lift over 110th Street, he emerged from the bathroom and sang his song, complex, continuous and whole. Robert had just enough energy left over from his night of trial to make love to me, despite his swollen gland, and then collapsed into a deep sleep on my mattress just as I, exhausted myself, had to get out of bed and get dressed to go to work.

We reached the kindergarten, I released my daughter's seat belt and she crawled over the transmission to kiss my cheek goodbye. Standing on the curb, the door still open, she turned to ask me if Robert was daddy's friend, too. I told her no.

Driving home, a tear formed in my eye and then rolled down my cheek. If my daughter had been there, she would have asked me if I was crying, and why, and I would have tried to explain to her that fullness of memory, as well as sorrow, can trigger tears. Are you hurt, Mommy? No. Yes. Only by the passage of time, my dear. Only by the terrible clarity of the illusion, that makes me feel the past must still exist somewhere, if only I could locate and reenter it.

It is too soon to ask myself if I would really like to enter that time again, or to live continuously with it, or if what might have happened would be in any way preferable to what actually has.

Robert's song, induced by guilt, was a refusal, a send up, a gutting obliteration of guilt. It is a bravely defiant song. The lyrics state all the reasons the singer has to feel guilty, and then denies them. The singer declares himself an outlaw, someone who lives outside the institutions that define morality and promise retribution for ignoring it. To oversimplify the past considerably: Robert and I were sleeping together, and the long years of Catholic boyhood (he was the brother marked from birth to be a priest) made him feel we shouldn't be.

If singing could make it so, if it really took only one night of trial to exorcise the godly demons, if the thing made could shape the life, then everything might be a good deal different now. My daughter, if I had one, would be black-haired and brown-eyed, not brown and blue, she would be ruddy-cheeked and long-boned, instead of elfin pale. I would not be this me but another. The lines on my face would lie differently and be more or less deep. Perhaps I never would have cut my long hair. I would dream different dreams at night.

It *is* an oversimplification. Before I met him, Robert was thinking of leaving the seminary. We met and he left. Some time after I left him, he returned and was on the point of ordination, only days away, when the letter I'd sent weeks before to a long superseded address finally reached him. He left again. I was not, as this makes me sound, a fickle and heartless intervenor between a man and his God. Just who and what I was is harder to remember. The monastic cell was not hospitable to rock-'n'-roll, but I helped his music flower. Besides, he told me that the first time we were together, he was burning more on ego than on love. He said he scarcely knew me— really— then. Which intelligence, even delivered long after the fact, hurt and baffled me. I'd thought he was my mirrored self, my soulmate. Actually, I think it's his memory that's faulty and not mine. I still believe we were.

All morning I kept the house radio on, tuned to the same station that had played Robert's song, even though the constant patter of the announcer distracted me from my work, and the blare of the commercials gnawed at my nerves. My aural vigilance was rewarded; twice more, I heard the song. I learned that it was "new" and growing popular. It was recorded, I learned, by a group named Goody Ten Shoes which, I deduced, must be a five-member band. Their arrangement leaned toward the country, with a lot of ham fat and too much reverb on the slide guitar.

Robert wrote his songs and performed them solo on a twelve-string guitar, but inside his head and implicit in the music was a hard-rock symphony. I could hear it, too, the sound as he imagined it, first because he worked so hard to suggest its richness and complexity with just two instruments, voice and guitar, and second, simply because I knew him very well. We had an empathetic access to each other's minds in those days. I could hear his piano, his bass, the drum solo, the saxophone and flute that spoke in the instrumental interlude. Robert wrote songs most often in a modified sonata form that allowed more for transformation than the simple repetitions of the ballad; in this song, in what he used to call "the bridge," the voice is supposed to soar into falsetto, into that thin, incandescent sound-place Robert found inside himself. Goody Ten Shoes didn't even try.

The *she* in the lyric is me, of course, or perhaps more accurately, was me. The woman in the next room, thought to be asleep. My hair no longer spills across the pillow the same way, and I doubt my husband would ever say I was soft as dawn or cool as a Sunday in spring. Who was she, anyway? Hearing the song, I felt that girl was lost, it made me desperate to find her.

I looked for her in my daughter, after I picked her up at school, and convinced myself there were resemblances, even though my daughter's face is still childishly round, her wrists and ankles braceleted with baby fat. Her skin is fine and cool, her cheeks flush prettily with the excitement of play. I cajoled her down to nap, then snuck in to watch her sleep, full of a great love that like the ocean, rose and broke in me. Broke harder than ever because, all morning, I'd allowed myself to imagine an alternate reality in which the existence of this precious daughter became impossible.

Of the woman in the song, I succeeded in remembering a few particulars:

1) That she too felt guilt. At being cast as the agent of separation, the other woman causing Robert to cheat on Mother Church, his mystical bride-to-be. The fact that she was an atheist, that she could smell the opiate in the incense and taste the poisons in the communion cup, did nothing to allay that guilt. She felt guilty too at not being the sort of girl that her mother wished her to be at this point in her life— clear-headed, successful, playing the field socially, pursuing her career. According to whichever canon, love was a heresy.

2) That she was frightened by the intensity of her relationship with Robert. He expected human love to be as all-consuming as divine. Perhaps, under the circumstances, he needed it to be that way, and it most often was. So that she felt they were living too fast, too deep, too bright. So that she began to fear the immolation of her separate self. Robert drew strength from her, as if she were a fuel. She began to wonder if her own peculiar resources were renewable or, if Robert were allowed to burn them, they would be spent.

3) That there was nothing ordinary, no dailiness, about their life together. It was all creation. Passion. Ecstasy. And guilt.

4) That she had to leave him.

5) That, even though she made mistakes after leaving him, that first time, leaving him was not a mistake.

At dinner, my daughter announced, "Mommy heard her friend on the radio today."

"What friend?" my husband asked.

"Her old friend," my daughter said, and above his plate, my husband looked to me for clarification. It was not that I didn't want to tell my husband about hearing Robert's song, but that I didn't want to tell him this way, so that it seemed important. I'd planned to tell him casually. One day, as I imagined it, we'd be driving in the car, and Robert's song would come on the radio. "Oh, by the way," I'd say, "that's Robert's song."

He waited for my answer. "Robert McElvey," I said. "You remember. The one who..."

"I remember," my husband said.

My husband and Robert met just once, in New York City. It was after I'd left Robert the second time and before my husband had any legal right to make moral claims on me, though I was pretty sure I loved him by that time. He'd gone to New York on business, and I accompanied him. While he kept his afternoon appointments, I met Robert in Washington Square Park, at the same bench near the fountain we'd always trysted on. It was late fall, all pale sun and blustery wind, the kind of New York day that lifts your spirits and stings your skin. Robert had on his old navy peacoat and his big brown boots, but there were streaks of white in his black hair and under the worn hippie vestments, he was wearing a black shirt and a clerical collar. By old habit, my body was drawn to his body, but his costume and the memory of my new lover's recent embrace censored attraction. We aborted the natural embrace and instead joined hands. Robert's eyelids were red near the lashes, the way they always got when the weather turned cold, and I was caught on the cusp of two feelings: I know this man as well as I know myself; this man is a stranger to me.

We tried to work the strangeness off by walking, by engaging our new selves in an old past-time. In the old days, we'd covered miles of Manhattan, of Brooklyn, of Robert's old stomping ground, the Bronx, lost in thought, in conversation, and in each other. Our gaits have always been well-matched, and we walk at the same fast pace when our minds are speeding. That day, we walked, all through the Village and then to midtown where, anomalously and as always, the presence of a cast of diverse thousands did not diminish but intensified our sense of private drama.

The wind made my eyes water, and I was constantly brushing away tears with my free hand. Robert held the other. At Rockefeller Plaza, he took me in his arms, he held me close and kissed me hard. I trembled from a strong sense of, not wrongness exactly, but of strangeness. I kissed him back, and could feel our bodies anticipating the next stage, the lovemaking we had so often permitted them and now would not. Robert's peacoat was open and there was nothing to keep me from feeling his excitement, or him, the readiness it roused in me.

It was the stares of passers-by, indignant, amused, some merely curious, that defined the moment for me: I was engaging in foreplay with a Roman Catholic priest in full public view. In that instant, I understood something important, if paradoxical, about the man: though Robert is unusually susceptible to guilt, he has no conscience.

"So," my husband said, "Mick Jagger of the Sacred Heart makes it at last."

I shrugged.

For a moment, watching us, our daughter looked puzzled. Then, unexcused, she got up from the table.

"Where do you think you're going?" my husband asked.

"To turn on the radio, so you can hear Mommy's old friend's song," our daughter said.

"Sit down and eat your dinner," my husband said.

"Don't you want to hear the song?" she asked him.

My husband said no.

Later that night, he spoke into the dark warm space between our pillows, a place so many words, significant and trivial, have passed across. "How did it make you feel to hear your old lover's song on the radio?"

I answered without hesitation. "Old. It made me feel old."

He laughed. "Is that all?"

"No," I said. "Of course not."

"Regrets?" he asked.

"Memories. I haven't thought about Robert for a long time. I didn't even answer his last letter."

"Is he here now?"

I shook my head in the darkness. "What you have to understand," I said, "is that it's also a way of remembering me."

"I don't have to understand anything," he said. He said it kindly, but he turned his back to me and pulled the covers up around him, foreclosing possibilities and at the same time, being delicate, letting me know he wouldn't intrude. I clung to him in the darkness, insisting there was no space between us.

That night, though, my dreams were a wedge. Robert was there, bent over his guitar, the curve of his black hair hiding one eye, the other closed as he sang. His chin sharpened, he wore a look of pain as he forced his voice high, higher, almost into the female registers; his skin seemed to strain to contain his skull, and then relaxed as he let his voice drop down again. All night his calluos-padded fingers played the strings and he sang me every song he ever wrote, for God or woman, and I listened, as I always have, transfixed, claimed and encircled by his music.

I am part of his music, variously the goddess, the temptress, the villain, the smile, the setting sun, the touch, the speaker, the object lost or found, the body, the pleasure or the pain that pushed him up, up into falsetto as well as the peace that mellowed him, the weight that pushed him down. I am the saxophone, the cymbals. I am his future and his past and when I woke in the morning, my hands had to reach out and read flesh before I knew for sure that the man who lay beside me was the same man, the only man who's been there in the morning these many years.

My husband got up, my daughter got up with him, and I heard him whisper, "Let Mommy sleep."

I floated in bed warmth, in that place where past and present are simultaneous possibilities, neither preclusive, until my husband kissed me goodbye and I got up to put on my clothes and my caretaker's role for the day.

Robert never understood why I left him the second time. For more than a year, we'd lived by choice in separate cities, and every two or three weeks, got together for a long weekend or a short week. His songs poured forth. Robert's first tutors had been the early Beatles, the Stones and their progenitors, Buddy Holly, and black midwestern blues. Now he began to study music in earnest, its theory and history, and the songs he wrote grew lyrically simpler and harmonically more sophisticated. More and more, he imposed classical form on rock intentions until I imagined that at the jam session in his head, Bach sat at the keyboard, Mozart in a sequined satin shirt played bass, Greg Allman or Larry Coryell guitar, that Louis Armstrong dropped in now and then for a trumpet solo, that Ringo Starr or Béla Bartók were equally welcome to take a lick on the drums. More than eclectic, his music grew synthetic and always, at the center of the fantasy was Robert, long-boned and shockingly thin, wearing his time-whitened blue jeans and his creator's arrogance, eyes closed

38

and lips trembling as he trilled his apocalyptic high notes into a microphone that fed an amplifier aimed directly and full volume at the human heart.

Things ostensibly were going well. My own work prospered, and our times together were rich in talk and touch. When he was there on weekdays and I had to work, Robert made the bed and shopped and cooked, vacuumed, took long walks and wrote songs. As a lover, he was vastly different from the first time, more melody and less percussion, but we still played well together, and in longer forms. When we were apart, we wrote and called each other frequently, and during the last of our shared interludes, we seriously discussed living in the same city, in the same apartment. The move seemed imminent.

To say I left him the second time because he gave me a dose of the clap is, once again, to simplify too much. We'd made no promises of fidelity and, while I have always been a serial monogamist, Robert wasn't. He played gigs in the coffee houses and hippie bars of the city where he lived, and I knew there was a coterie, small but willing, of Robert McElvey groupies who followed his career and sometimes were rewarded for their loyalty by a visit to his bed. He never slept all night with them, he told me; that was his bottom line, his proof of love, and at the time, it seemed sufficient.

Which brings me to another insight about the past: I must have been willing to share Robert because exclusive possession of him would have been too burdensome. Possessing, I would have been possessed. So the clap was probably only an excuse, except insofar as it symbolized Robert's chronic impracticality, his way of doing what he wanted with no real understanding that effects have causes, and the reverse. He was always too willing to leave the logistics to someone else, to slip out when it was time to clean up after the party. Call it the clap.

My daughter is unusually sensitive to my states of mind. When she feels I am fragile, she trades roles with me, becomes the comforter and giver. Sometimes her solicitude precedes my understanding of myself, her gentleness and concern tell me I'm off my feed emotionally. It happened that way that morning, the morning after I heard Robert's song. She climbed on my lap and patted my hair, she stroked my cheek and looked searchingly into my eyes. Her little girl voice parodied mine, octaves lower, giving solace. "It's okay, Mommy. It really is okay."

She may have meant one thing was okay, and I another. She may have meant, "It's okay to be sad or wistful about what's past, Mom," while I took her words to be permission, from the innocent source, to continue imagining my alternate reality, parallel because possible, to the one we both inhabited. As I did so, the imaginary present held the real one in abeyance, they achieved a kind of parity, which meant that I both lived in and regretted each; I occupied a simultaneous duality that so stretched my emotional capacity I felt my body must be expanding with it, getting ready to burst.

The night my husband and Robert and I met for dinner in New York was the hardest time I ever remember experiencing, not because they weren't eminently civilized— they were— but because I, my emotional protoplasm, stretched so elastically between them. I identified entirely with each; I was his perfect mate— my competent, impatient, world-saving husband; my spiritual, insubstantial, impractical priest. The man who walked a hard road steadily; the man who flew and sometimes crashed. The man who shepherded; the one who burned. Earth and ether. I was both and I knew it was impossible to be both. What I felt was not fullness but threatening division. What I feared was splitting, as an atom does, the swift and terrible explosion, the conversion of matter to energy. I feared that transformation. I was afraid to cease to be.

Robert and my husband conversed, explored each other's resumes and discovered points of common interest; they ate food and drank wine, laughed and even ventured, politely, to disagree, while I clawed at the walls of the cyclotron, trying to brake the speed I travelled down that dark tunnel toward oblivion. I survived the evening only by long and frequent visits to the ladies' room, by breathing my way deep and slowly into a meditation that had no object, a kind of self-willed catatonia. At the end of the evening, the two men shook hands, Robert brushed his lips lightly against my cheek, a butterfly's goodbye, and my husband took me firmly by the arm and guided me back to our hotel room. I have walked with him ever since, I've held that arm.

My daughter turned on the radio. They were playing Robert's song, and inside, around the amiable baritone of Goody Ten Shoes' lead singer, I could hear Robert's voice calling me. He was God's by default. He would forgive the last letter, unanswered for a year, he would forgive everything. Our story never ended, but was only interrupted. I had only to speak the word. Speak the word only. Speak, and his soul would be mine. His voice was beautiful. It was high and full of pain. His voice was seductive with need and promise. It was the ultimate love song, a siren song that tingled every nerve, flared every synapse in me.

I gathered my daughter on my lap and held her tightly, felt her sturdy little body in my arms and her soft breath on my cheek, while I closed my eyes against visions and the tears came anyway. I didn't plug my ears, couldn't, because the song was playing in me, was part of me. I lashed myself to my daughter, listened and suffered until we sailed past danger, and the radio stopped playing Robert's song.

Dreams of a New Mother

BIRTH IS inconvenient, incomplete, unjust, an imperfect separation. Once you rode together through the nights and days, the flexing of her toes a tickle inside your ribs, her twists and squirms a mute communication, reassurance that you prospered jointly, your welfares utterly congruent. Now you are here and she is there. She sleeps and you do not. You listen to her sleep. The slightest of her sighs sets off sirens deep in your brain. You chase molecules across the ceiling, imaginary flecks of moving black, run the sheep backwards, toward wakefulness, forbid yourself to be seduced by the silent warmth of the husband who sleeps beside you, or lulled by the long, slow rhythm of his breaths. Sternly forbid yourself the pleasures of the deep, kind bed and smooth sheets, refuse to board the nightlong, headlong brainvacation train that races by so fast it makes a wind that brushes your cheek in the dark. You must not, dare not board and ride, because your baby sleeps in her crib a million miles away across

the room and must not wake to find you gone. Kinetically familiar, she is visually new, unimaginably small. Her needs are
simple and immense. She was born holding your heart in her
hands, clutching your nerves like reins in her tiny fists.

You must not dare not must not dare not must not dare not
long to need to ache to absolutely must not dare not will not sleep.

The meat is red and raw, oozing beef blood, a large, crude
roast you clutch in sticky hands. The boy tries to take it by force.
Larger than you, he is still growing, devours everything in sight
to fuel the last push into manhood. You fight bitterly, this bloody
hunk of protein the prize. He wants it to grow, you need it to
survive. All bonds are broken, all bets off. You are both beyond
sharing. There is no love in your heart, and none in his eyes. He
grabs your arm and twists it painfully behind you, while you kick
and claw without restraint, trying to reimburse him pain for
pain.

The baby cries. You wake and rise to feed her. Only her body
wakes this time. Her eyelids are puckered shut and she sucks
blindly at your breast.

You recant before the testimony of your senses. The house
exists. The ruddy mantlepiece and gray-pink rug, the round pink
ottoman whose rolling you rode as a child. Familiar scent of
pomander, of dusty rose, old wool, false leather, burning wood,
and walnut oil to make the baby grand piano shine. The china
dog and burnished vase are safe upon their shelf. Your mother is
not dead. If you can find her and apologize for the misappre-
hension of death, she will not die to you again. Your baby lives,
and needs your milk to go on living. It is long and dangerously
past her feeding time and she screams with hunger, somewhere
out of sight. Two lives to save, and you must answer for two
deaths, rooted here in sensuous memory, trapped between genera-
tions, unable to move.

The baby cries. You wake and rise to feed her. In the nest of her covers, with her thin neck and ruffled hair, she is a small bird, angry at her hunger. Crying. Until you feed her and she sleeps again.

The baby bites your nipple off and spits it out in the dusty corner behind your rocking chair. Blood pours from the wound, and you are paralyzed by hurt. The baby howls in rage at the red milk that flows so fast and tastes so salty strange until, infinitely adaptable, she rallies and learns to drink your blood.

The baby cries. You wake and rise to feed her. The sky has just begun to lighten behind the blind, and in the grainy bedroom light, you can see her one-eyed sideways blue stare above your breast, hunger even more intense than love.

She is lost through your fault, your own most grievous fault. You were living your life, in the midst of doing something that gave you minor pleasure, gossiping or talking politics, and you forgot, misplaced her. Where? It is hours since she ate. Your breasts are throbbingly full. The laughter of children leads you to a bedroom with a triptych mirror above the dresser, a mahogany bedstead dark and solemn as a grave. There on the bed, a small boy lies beside your child, cradling her close the way it warms your heart and sweetens motherhood to do. Around the bed, a line of children coils, watching and waiting to sleep beside the babe. Each gives you fifty sticky palm-warm cents to pay for the privilege that should be yours alone, to nestle the tiny body soft and damp and limp with sleep.

The baby cries. You wake and rise to feed her. After she is settled in your arms and sucking, you raise the blind a cautious inch or two to watch how morning whitens the bay, the mountain and the dunes, a thousand childish pines calligraphed black on the rice paper sky. You stroke the baby's downy head. Sleep, love.

The young man wants you. It is no mockery. You are worth

45

wanting, young yourself, and slim, hair flowing to your waist, your breasts an ornament, belly flat and pale and luminous as morning on the river. Your hands are young, your throat young, eyes clear, thighs firm, wrists young, knees young, ears young, ankles and toes and waist young, lust young. You have a mother and are not a mother. The young man's touch is radiant over your buttocks, across the curved space of your back.

The baby cries. You wake and rise to feed her. Across the room, the man in the bed artlessly unfurls his naked limbs, sighs, ascending toward daytime, anticipating the summons of the clock that will make him disappear. Covers kicked away, you see his chest, where you want to rest your head, the arms, sleep-sprawled, you want to feel around you, and will the baby to eat fast so you can go to him and be with him a moment, only that, before he leaves.

The clock goes off. The man obeys it, emptying your bed, and there is no time for mothering of mothers, for the touching of fathers.

You rock in your chair beside the window and feed the child until she sleeps.

New Bed

THE SHADES still seal the room in dimness. When she opens her own eyes, Althea reads the shades; rectangles of light framed and crossed by bars of shadow from the windowpanes tell her the sun has risen, burned off the challenge of morning clouds and plans to shine all day. In this country, in June, the sun is often foiled. The white mist eats it for lunch and spends whole days digesting. Sometimes you can feel the sun lying in wait behind the haze, so that the mist is striated with geometric rays.

It is about six-thirty now; the clock confirms the light. Althea climbs out of bed to raise the shades, then comes back to lie on top of the covers. Just for a moment. The light begets an urgency and she is not, by nature, self-indulgent. Jacob's bed is made as neatly as one can be in the dark, in silence, so as not to wake a fellow sleeper, blankets and spread pulled up to the pillows to hide the intimacy of naked sheets. In a few minutes, she will make her own bed and finish his.

Her body has no complaints this morning— no headache dawning, no backache lingering; no muscles strain to make her appreciate their past heroics. The air, on her naked arms, filtering through her thin nightgown, is warm-and-cold, sensual. It wakes her nerves, and she feels as if she's been dipped in honey, like a donut. She stretches and enjoys it, feels a tightness like longing in her thighs. She points her toes and tenses her legs again and again, feels the tightness travel like electric current the length of her legs and finds some kind of release in the final upward flex of ankle.

While she is not thinking about her hands, they move quietly, without delay, to cup one breast, to rub against the thatch that lifts the nightgown a little up from skin and bone. An itch, she tells herself sternly when she discovers it, then lets her fingers linger, to scratch some more. She is careful not to look at her body. Without mirrors, it is possible to remember, to trust the continuity of sensation without the reprimand of physical change.

For Jacob, there can be no leisured wakings, no flirtation with the morning light. Up at three, shocked out of sleep by an alarm that sounds, deliberately, like danger, he is all awake at once, carrying no baggage from his dreams, forgetting in the first instant of waking where he has spent the night. Sometimes she is tempted to inspect his sheets for signs of nighttime passion— it was easy to see on the boys' sheets as they slipped into manhood— but always she restrains herself; it would be too big a breach of his privacy, of the privacy they grant each other.

Althea gets up and finds her glasses on the nightstand. The world snaps into focus; the shadows lose their soft edges and become crisp lines obeying some material logic she perceives and does not question.

In the bathroom, she takes her glasses off again and sets them on the back of the toilet. Her face is grateful for the water she splashes on it, soothed by the white lotion she rubs until it disappears. There is no time or need for makeup now. Such artifice belongs to afternoons, and she looks forward to the feel of sun on her naked face. It should not have to burn through paints and powders, and she is philosophical about freckles, remembers her mother's admonition to wear a sun hat always, her mother's disapproval of tanned and spotted skin.

"We are not farmers," her mother said. "The sun will make you old before your time."

But Althea was not careful. Her girlhood was a stream of straw hats laid aside and lost, hems torn, white dresses soiled with adventure. She loves the sun with the same simple passion her garden does.

In the instant she sees phlox and mint, sweet pea and lavender, daffodils, pansies, chives and thyme in her mind, she knows the point of this slow waking. She knows how she will spend her day.

Jacob's breakfast dishes are on the table, a quiet piece of domestic art that reminds her of the living man. For twenty-five years now she's found these artifacts each morning, puzzled out his menu and his mood by their position and the few discreet crumbs he leaves behind. He had oatmeal again, and doused it with maple syrup, toast (the crumbs lie in a little blot of condensation on the plate).

He's left the coffeepot half-full, as always, so she need only reheat it for herself. She puts his dishes in the sink and realizes she will not do them right away. Through the window over the sink, she sees her garden bloom. It calls to her. Coffee will be enough this morning. The pot rattles on the burner with the excitement of being hot.

She takes her own place at the table and lets the coffee cool again while she appreciates the quiet of the house. There is never more than a little traffic on the road, and the appliances respect the silence, coughing rarely, stirring only slightly in their mechanical sleep. Nothing will ever be again as noisy as the children were. Even when they went to school, their noise remained, the sound of their toys, missing them, the silence too interim to take power, bracing itself for their return. Now she can trust it to remain.

She and Jacob are catlike in their living, their movements sure, their spates of conversation so soft and regular that it's hard to remember, after, if one has spoken out loud. At night, the news announcer talks while she cooks, but talks to Jacob only. For her, he is only a subliminal hum behind the voices of the spoons and pans.

On a peg in the garage she finds them, a pair of overalls so old they no longer crackle and crease but, their fibers pounded and broken by years of wear and washing, lie against the skin like flannel, no stranger to the body or the world but an intermediary between them, minimizing distinctions. Praise be to J.C. Penney. The overalls are ancient but clean— the dirt and paint and oil of countless tasks worked into the fabric— become part of the design.

She carries them back to the bedroom and finds an old shirt, red, in the back of her closet. By habit, she snatches up a brassiere, but when she holds it up to make sure it's right side out, it suddenly becomes an alien device, designed to perform feats of reconstruction that nature laughs at. Althea is fifty-one years old, and her breasts are happy to lie back against her body and rest. The have suckled two children, men now, with children of their own. In her days of having beaux, Althea was most often called statuesque, a strapping woman. Lean Jacob's overalls fit nicely, save for the legs, which she rolls up three turns to equalize the difference between Jacob's body and her own.

Her hair is getting long again, the permanent grown out.

Twice a day, she notices this. Brushing through the chemical frizz, she thinks obediently, I should call Len and make an appointment for a permanent, then subdues the wayward hair with bobby pins and a bandana. It will take a wedding in the family or a tea she has to pour to drive her to the beauty shop with its evil smells and gossiping women, to the long slow torture of the dryer.

It is not silent outside the house. Drunk on sunshine, the world is garrulous. Out of loyalty and long habit, she visits the vegetables first, but her love for them is partial. They are Jacob's beets and carrots, Jacob's cukes and peas, lettuce and cabbage and peppers, gifts he brings her. She is only their guardian in his absence. She works a rich mixture of coffee grounds and egg shells in around the carrots and beets, until the grainy brown grounds are indistinguishable from the soil and the shells become only splinters of white, like flecks of stone in the brown dirt. The wind starts a rumor and it spreads through the beans; the foolish brief white blossoms nod as they receive the news, whistle softly, pass it on.

Althea ties up an escaping tendril or two with string, plucks out a weed or two grown since the weekend. Behind the garden, Jacob's crop of pine stands watch, a vegetable army, arrayed in rows. He calls them the start of a Christmas Tree Farm, a hedge against inflation, a new career, when he retires from the bakery. That he will ever cut them down she doubts. Men need excuses for their tenderness.

The bees have started work earlier than she, coaxing the nectar from sweet pea and snapdragon. Tanked up, they fly off dizzy home to blow the fumes of their intoxication at other, hive-bound bees. It does not seem that they should be able to fly at all, with their fat elliptical bodies, their absurdly tiny wings, the dirigibles of insectdom. As a child, she envied them. Now she is convinced it is their buzz that keeps them airborne, that a con-

tinual series of tiny beefarts jets them back and forth. Sometimes still she dreams of flying.

She does routine things first, the maintenance, snaps off past
blossoms, pulls up the weeds, so new and tender now they don't
seem noxious, and she feels a little guilty uprooting them. The
dirt pales as it dries, the ridges first, and she waters gently. Often,
she interrupts herself to chew a sprig of mint, to crush a few small
blossoms of lavender against her palm to free their scent. She
spends time with the pansies, her favorites, peering into their
velvety faces, wishing, almost, they would speak, for what the
pansies said would surely be worth knowing.

She would like to ask them what it feels like to have roots, a
dark side, hidden below ground, searching, what an earthworm
feels like, tunneling through root hairs, what it is to smell sweet
and die soon. Compared to them, she is perennial, her cycle long,
measured in gardens that grow and die.

The sun climbs, moves around the garden. Watercan in hand,
she follows it. She finds a hummingbird, his needle beak inserted
in a foxglove blossom. His body beats so fast it seems motionless,
his wings visible only as a fluttering of light. Her own body tries
to imagine what it is like to burn so bright. The doctors gave her
digitalis once, and it felt like the onset of fear. Where is it in the
plant? To accelerate the hummingbird's heart would be to murder
it; it would simply explode into the sunlight, leaving no residue.

Wheels crunch the gravel drive out front. It does not alarm
her. She waits to hear the engine find reverse and leave; their
driveway is the only turnaround in a mile. The hummingbird
takes his fill and darts away, wings beating sunlight. The engine
dies. It does not sound like a delivery truck.

She plunges her trowel into the dirt again, detects a stone and
digs for it with her fingers. Her friends will know where to find
her. If it is someone from the Garden Club, she will understand

the overalls. To someone from the Eastern Star, she might have to explain, or even apologize a little: "I'm sure I look a fright."

She keeps on digging, waiting for a figure to round the corner of the house and turn familiar. What is there for lunch? If it's someone she likes, Althea will invite her to stay.

But no one rounds the corner. No engine starts and drives away. It must be a Fuller Brush man, an Avon lady, a Jehovah's Witness beating the bushes for fresh souls. These she is willing to miss. Let them think she isn't home. Her trowel unearths a worm, long as a bracelet if you wound him end to end, pinkly pearled. His blind snout pushes against the air and finds it no obstacle. She watches him twist and slither, exploring for a point of re-entry into the earth. He pushes in, dragging his body behind him.

Still her unseen visitor has not appeared or given up. The door's unlocked. She remembers the television set, and her mother's silver, on display in the china closet, imagines a thief stalking through the house, taking his pleasure with their possessions— the toaster, the radio, the wedding locket nestled on cotton in a little box on the dresser— perhaps so bold, so sure of his security he opens up the icebox and treats himself to lemon pie or last night's meatballs. Which china will he use to serve himself, and will he take that, too?

Althea rises from her gardener's crouch. The trowel balances nicely in her hand; she could strike with it, if necessary, and her garden gloves would leave no prints. Yet it must, she thinks, be legal to hit someone who's stealing your mother's silver teapot; surely no jury would be hard on you for that. It is a lovely teapot, standing on viny Victorian feet, its handle bumpy in your hand with silver roses.

She wishes Jacob were home. He could sneak into the garage and load his .22. Althea has never loaded a gun in her life, never fired one. She wishes for some weapon more menacing than her trowel. The hoe will let her keep her distance when she strikes; she finds it leaning against the house like a laconic workman and picks it up. Thus armed, trowel and hoe held tight and ready, she walks quietly as she can around the house, staying off the flag-stones where her shoes will sound and keeping to the softer sur-face of the lawn.

The man is still on the porch, fist drawn back for another barrage of knocks no one will hear. He is wearing a suit and looks no more criminal than Richard Nixon did. He doesn't hear her coming till she speaks.

"Can I help you with something?" she asks.

"Is this the Jacob Hanson residence?" His voice is polite and polished as his gray suit. She sees he has no bag, no vacuum cleaner.

"It is," she says. "But if you're selling something, we don't want it. The vacuum works and we got more magazines than we can read."

"I've nothing to sell." He smiles. "I'm looking for Mrs. Hanson."

"You've found her." Her voice is suspicious, a little defiant even. She leans on the hoe, the trowel still ready in her hand.

"Althea, of course!" he says. Then, "Let me take a look at you."

His stance is no longer apologetic as he moves toward her. His arms swing freely at his sides, and he looks like a TV producer's idea of a professional man, slim and confident, still youthful despite gray hair and (maybe) dentures.

Instinctively, she raises the trowel a little. It stops him short. "What do you want with me?" Jacob takes care of the insurance through the Lodge. Whatever he's selling must be expensive to turn him out so well.

He laughs, and there is something familiar about the laugh

that makes her wary and curious all at once. "What's funny?" she demands. "This is private property, you know, and you're trespassing."

"And you're about to run me off. My God. You always did have spunk."

He claims to know her. Something in her brain ignites and burns backward, through closed passages, back. How far must she travel to find him? He is no one from the recent past.

"I'm sorry. I should have called first. I don't know why I didn't."

The fuse still smolders, close to the explosives now. "Who are you?" she asks.

And as she asks, she knows. Some movement of his head or hands, some vision completed ignites her memory. They say it together, "Ben Taylor."

With recognition comes embarrassment. She drops the hoe and trowel and wraps her arms around her, wishing she had enough hands to hide the overalls, her body, her face and head.

"I was working in the garden. It's such a beautiful day."

"I guessed."

"I don't normally go around the house like this."

"You look fine. I should have called first."

"It's nice to see you. Have you had lunch?"

He looks at his watch, an expensive watch, decorative. Jacob still carries a pocket watch. "It is almost noon. But I didn't mean to invite myself for a meal. I would have been earlier, but it took me awhile to find Beaver Lane."

"Well, now you're here, you may as well stay and eat."

Althea peels off her garden gloves and turns, to lead him to the kitchen door. This morning, of all, she has not done the breakfast dishes. She stamps her brown oxfords on the rubber welcome mat to shake off dirt and Ben, behind her, stops to wipe his shiny city shoes.

"Come in, come in," she calls. "I'll put the kettle on."

She gets him seated, taking Jacob's chair, and makes him tea. His eyes follow her around the kitchen.

"Can you wait a few minutes?" she asks. "I'd like to get cleaned up and change."

"Don't bother on my account. I didn't come to cause you trouble."

"No trouble. Just some lipstick anyway. I bet you never catch your wife without her lipstick."

She heard, of course, when he got married, but did not hear to whom, or what she was like. A girl from California, they said, with some money.

"Ruth is dead," he says. "But no, I never did."

"I'm sorry, Ben." In the pause, she studies his face, then laughs, trying to turn it around. "Wouldn't you know it? An old beau comes to call and finds me in overalls."

"It's good to see you," Ben says. "I don't mind the clothes."

"I do." She leaves him in the kitchen and runs to the bathroom, washes her hands and scrubs her nails, undoes the bandana and wrestles her hair into a tentative French roll that may stay pinned if she can remember not to move her head too much. She puts on lipstick. In her closet, she reaches for her best dress, then grows self-conscious. She lives in the country. This is her home, and she doesn't dress up here, not usually. She will not do for Ben what Jacob doesn't ask. She takes slacks and shirt from their hangers and puts them on— nice shirt, nice slacks.

The mirror tells her she looks like herself. There is no time now to undo fifty years of sunshine, a husband and two sons.

She comes back to find him browsing through a mail order catalog from a nursery down in Oregon. "They make purple roses now," he says.

Althea nods. "I hate them. They look unnatural."

56

He closes the catalog and smiles at her, so that she feels her lipstick must be smeared, her French roll falling down already.

She retreats to the refrigerator and peers inside. At least she can make up in cooking what she's lost in looks. There is a little casserole, thawed and ready for the oven, half a molded salad from Tuesday's Garden Club luncheon, a lemon pie. He watches her fuss in the kitchen, offers once to help. She tells him to sit still.

"Actually, I've become a pretty good cook since Ruth passed on," he says.

Finally they're settled face to face at the table. She has to look at him. Now it seems impossible that she failed to recognize him; he's aged much the way she used to imagine he would, back when she had a stake in imagining such things. That she is not at all as she imagined she would be hits home. There was no nursing school and no career, only babies and clubs and pies. Her failures make her shy. He seems so prosperous.

"My god, it's good to see you," he says. "I hope you don't mind if I stare."

Althea blushes. He asks about her family, and she recites their histories, glad not to have to talk about herself, trying hard to remember high school grammar and avoid the lapses she's adopted— no ain'ts, no don'ts where none belong. He speaks so well.

"Thank you for sending flowers when Mother died. How did you know?"

"Oh, I still keep up with a few folks around here. They have orders to keep me up to date on you."

She parries. "Do you have children?"

"Only one. A daughter. She's married now, to a gynecologist in San Diego. Not my idea of the ideal job, but he likes it and she likes him." He shrugs.

"Grandchildren?"

"Not yet. Jennie just finished nursing school and got married last June. I got married quite awhile after you did, you know. I had a broken heart to mend."

"Ben Taylor, you're as full of moonbeams as you always was. You went away."

"You told me to."

"I didn't tell you to go to San Francisco. You never wrote me."

"I did. Religiously. You never answered."

"You wrote?"

"Every day for months."

"You must not have mailed them, then. I asked for letters every day."

"At the post office?"

"From Rudy. Rudy used to get the mail on his way home."

"Rudy never liked me. He must have thrown them away. Burned them, maybe." Ben laughs, but his eyes are serious.

"Rudy wouldn't do a thing like that."

"I wrote the letters," Ben says. "I mailed them."

"He wouldn't." In a family of nine, there's bound to be an odd one. With them, it was her brother Rudy, a stringy boy with fierce eyes and rusty hair. He never married. Worked in a bank, until they accused him of taking money. Then he threw himself off a bridge, into a river that still flows by the family home. "I can no longer live with this guilt," he wrote. The casket was closed at the funeral. The bank sent an enormous wreath, having found the missing money. Rudy was guilty of poor arithmetic, nothing more. What guilt, they asked themselves, what guilt, and slowly came to believe he was unbalanced, willing to assume the guilt the bank demanded.

"He didn't like me," Ben insists. "Look here." He half stands up, takes his wallet out of his hip pocket and opens it, unfolding an accordian of plastic cards. He pulls out a Shell credit card and digs for something behind it. Ben hands her a picture of herself, the whites gone beige with age, the edges tattered. Her own imp's face, the hair piled high, the flowing body and high, firm bosom. She turns it over to find the inscription she remembers writing— *For Ben With All My Love, Althea.* The hand is confident, sure he would come back, sure she would be ready when he did.

"I do remember," she says.

But thirty years have made a stranger of him. Their lives' divergence is complete. He wears cuff links, his hands are soft. Something beyond prosperous— he looks important, as though he's used to talking to governors and having his picture in the paper.

Althea laughs. "Maybe Rudy did us both a favor." The pain is gone, but the scar tissue has long been a part of her. She would feel regret if she could.

"I doubt it," he says. "It took me four years to get over you."

"And those four years are part of you. They make you what you are. And I'm sure you finally did much better for yourself. Can you imagine me a lawyer's wife?"

"Of course. I often have. Especially since Ruth died." He leans toward her a little. "Are you happy, Althea?"

It is not a question she asks herself, not a question people she knows ask themselves. Ben seems handsome but unreal, like the characters that Cary Grant plays in the movies.

"Does Jacob make you happy?" She can hear the lawyer in his voice now, imagines herself on the witness stand. Accepting the onus of the oath, she tries to answer truthfully.

"A lot of things make me happy," she says. "And Jacob doesn't make me unhappy. We get along."

"I'm sorry, Althea."

"What on earth for?" No fancy lady, but she has her pride.

She won't apologize for Jacob, whose overalls she wears, or for herself, who wears them.

"We could have done so much together."

"Could, would. It's water over the dam, Ben. And it don't flow backwards."

"No." He picks a slice of bread off the plate and butters it. Most of it he eats in silence, then asks, "Did you make this? It's delicious."

"Jacob did. That's Romanoff's. He's head baker now. He mixes all the rye and sourdough himself. They say there's none does better."

He finishes the bread. "Proud Althea, a baker's wife."

"I'm not ashamed of what my husband does."

"No, you wouldn't be. Perhaps it was that partisanship I wanted for myself."

To cheer them both, she says, "I bet you've got quite a practice by now. You've really made it big, I hear."

"Don't believe everything you hear, Althea. But yes, I'm doing well. In September, I'm going to Europe again."

"Business or pleasure?"

"Both. Remember how we used to dream about going to live in Paris, France?"

"Sure." She smiles. "I never made it. Maybe someday before I die."

Ben folds his napkin neatly beside his plate. "Well, I've imposed myself on you long enough. I've got a five o'clock flight."

"You're welcome to wait here. Jacob will be home in a little while."

"No, I'll hit the road. I have to turn the car in, and check my bags." Ben stands up and his trousers fall into place above his shoes. It occurs to her he must have a dozen suits this good.

"I'll walk you to your car."

He heads for the kitchen door, but she diverts him: "No, use this one." She herds him toward the front and formal entrance. There is some elegance, some order in her life. She wants him to see the front room beyond the entry hall, with its proper and impassive chairs, the plushy sofa, the spotless carpet and the dustless lovely things that live there.

She watches his gaze enter and assess the room, linger on the old flocked velvet family album, a crewel cushion, the matching lamps on matching tables. It has never been her favorite room. She wishes now there were fresh flowers in it— there, on the round oak table. He turns back to her. His eyes study her, and she wonders what he sees.

"It's been good to see you again, Althea," he says. "I'm glad you're doing well." He rocks a little on his feet, toward the door, his voice a farewell.

Her sense of loss is strong enough to make her put a shy hand on his arm. It is the first time they've touched in thirty years. "Would you like to see my garden?" It is the first thing she can think of to hold him here. He may not care about flowers, but she wills him to care enough to ask her to look at them. In the absence of her children, not there to show him, it is her great accomplishment. She wants him to see how the flowers bloom for her, to smell how sweet the phlox is. The beds are her design, each plant a patient coaxed to life from seed or bulb.

"Why sure," he says, and for a moment touches the hand on his arm. She leads him out.

"It's not much, I suppose, but I love it."

Ben turns slowly to inspect the whole, then studies each bed, naming plants or asking names, touching a leaf here, a petal there, with a reverence that rewards and frightens her. He smiles at the pansies, plucks a sprig of mint and bruises it, to smell. Small wild red roses cascade over the trellis, perfuming the air, and Ben stops to touch a blossom.

"May I pick it?"

"Go ahead. There's plenty." Althea laughs. To want her rose is a delicious compliment. Here, among the flowers, she can remember Ben. He often made her laugh. "You really did write?" It seems important now.

He snaps a tiny thorn from the rose's stem. "Of course I did. You broke my heart, Althea." He says it easily, with no recrimination, so she can say, "I cried for nights, Ben. I couldn't understand."

Ben laughs and approaches her warily, as he would a strange dog or cat, to give no alarm. She stands still as he raises his arms, in slow motion, and works the stem of the rose into her hair, above the ear. "There," he says. "I'd really better go."

Side by side, they complete their circle of the house and end beside his car, a lush metallic Oldsmobile that seems too big for the driveway. He gets in.

"If I send you a Christmas card, will you write back?" He turns the key and the engine wakes and purrs.

"Of course," she says..

"Then *au revoir,* " he says. "Be well." He moves the shift stick and car springs forward, ready.

"Safe journey."

He lifts the brake and car eases away, fast and quiet. She waves at its receding trunk, rolling his French farewell around her tongue.

She clears their dishes from the table and adds them to the stack in the sink. Carefully she hangs her shirt and slacks back in the closet and puts on Jacob's overalls again.

Tired of maintenance, she decides to dig a new bed. She turns over earth, as careful as she can be not to bisect earthworms with the trowel blade. She plucks the stones out with her fingers, kneads the dirt with naked hands. The soil is dark and rich and full of promise. What she will plant there, she does not know.

Jacob's pickup throws gravel, coming in, and for awhile she waits for him to come and find her, ears turned to his footsteps, the skin on the back of her neck expectant. He does not come. Enough time passes that she knows he's gone straight to bed. She keeps on digging.

When the bed is done, edged in aluminum, inviting, she gets up and brushes the dirt from her knees.

Jacob's cryptic note on the refrigerator reads, "I've gone to bed. Please wake me for the news." He writes it out fresh every time. Sometimes she wonders why he doesn't save it and use it over and over again.

His body is buried in blankets, head covered with the pillow when she goes in, quietly, to change. The shades are drawn. She stands still until she can hear the sound of his breathing, watches till she can see the soft slight rise of the blankets. She will not wake him. Once he mutters something, and she freezes, one leg in her slacks, one poised above the leg hole, to hear, but the sound dies without making sense.

It is five o'clock. She takes the rose out from behind her ear and puts it in water in a shot glass on the window sill, then settles down with the seed catalog and a cup of tea.

Soon it will be time to start their supper.

The White Impala

BIRDSONG BEGINS it. It is a good door and almost always open. The city is full of birds. They sing continuously, but most of the time I don't hear them. I have about ninety seconds to make it through the door, and if I can't get there, then the run is likely to be a failure and a chore. A lot of things have to happen in those ninety seconds— the yammering in my head has got to stop, I have to banish tension from my muscles and relax my right knee so the hairline fracture in it doesn't hurt while I run, I have to loosen the knots in my stomach and forget about bill collectors, my mother's expectations, my daughter's nightmares.

When it works, there comes a lightening— the air is less resistant to my body, the blacktop kinder to my feet and ankles. The birds and the breezes in the leaves of the trees speak to me and I can understand their languages, or maybe more accurately, understand that it isn't important if I understand or not.

If the door slams on me before I manage to slip through it, then my breath will come hard and my legs will be lazy. My knee will throb and may falter. The voices of my kin will nag me. My shoulders will stay as tight as the mainspring of an overwound wrist watch. My will will fail me on an uphill grade, I'll stop running and walk home, ashamed of my weakness, feeling like shit. Even my sweat will smell different then, sharp and nervous and defeated.

Running is supposed to feel good, and if I can get through the door, it does. A robin calls. A jay. A nesting swallow scolds me. I listen to their chirping, ride the trills. My legs fall into rhythm. I shake my hands and rotate my shoulders, send a loving message to my right knee. The smells encroach, evergreen tang, must of cedar, rose breath, the diesel fart of an unseen bus. A police siren whines and I almost lose it— then, *one two three four*, I get it back. Concentrate on breathing, opening my lungs to the world. They expand and seem willing to function, though the exhaust fumes make them cringe a little. The first intersection is clear as I approach it. My stride lengthens, evens out. The first of the street signs passes by. *Siskiyou.* That's Indian. I don't know what it means.

I'm here, but here is always tentative. A song begins to sing itself, old Motown. Sometimes when I'm here, my brain sings scat. My brain has a lovely voice, rich and sexy. The voice that comes out of my mouth when I open it to sing has trouble staying on key. *The Tracks of My Tears* takes me past Stanton. The biker who swoops around the corner has a Walkman on his handlebars and wears earphones. He nods and I flutter back a smile that won't disrupt my breathing.

Here is easier and easier to reach. When I was six months pregnant, my thigh joints, just where they join the pelvis, began to feel imprecise and unreliable, and I stopped running regularly. At eight months, I ran a mile, just to see what it would feel like. It felt strange. I thought the baby was going to bypass normal channels, detour the unready cervix, crack the bottom of my convex belly and drop out on the cinder track. I thought that after I delivered, running would be very hard.

The German shepherd snarls a caution, but does not step beyond the edges of her lawn. Discipline, not rope, holds her. She seems to understand the street is public. Lets me pass. I feel a twinge in my right knee and try to suppress it.

It was surprising. More than a third of a year off, estranged from practice, after labor, delivery, recovery, and I put on my blue shoes and ran three miles. I ran them fast, almost effortlessly. Birth taught me stamina. I was, I *am* much stronger than ever I imagined; my body found that out and told my mind.

My body is warming, though I haven't broken sweat yet, and there is a core of languor, quite delicious, inside my effort. The rhythms of running remind me of rhythms of sex and I conjure a candlelit bedroom, bay-scented, a double bed and my husband on it. This is both memory and fantasy, what has happened, what will again. Then sometimes I think of all the young men I would have if I were not so married, or not so faithful, or not so old, or not so timid, or not myself, and thinking of them in this way seems to satisfy my lust for them and makes it easier to know that I'll not have them.

A bus crosses the intersection, heading east, and its leftside eyes stare at me. To the passengers, I am part of the landscape, slightly more interesting than an oak tree, because I move, less so than cherry or dogwood, because I do not bloom. The city is full of runners. We study, acknowledge, and salute when we meet each other in the streets.

The growl of the bus engine recedes and for a moment, even the birds are silent, then a lawnmower chortles. Then a plane. Then I can smell the leveled grass. The plane has drawn a vapor trail between me and the sun. It fattens, blurs, but doesn't disappear. The plane has scratched the sky and the wound, though minor, is slow to heal. Proud flesh of clouds. I close my eyes and see sunspots against my red lids, then the darkness becomes personal, sharpening my other senses. Grass, birds, wind. Passing under the tall elms and chestnuts, I feel the pattern of hot and cool they and the sun conspire to draw against my skin.

When I open my eyes, it's there, an image from old dreams: white Chevrolet, Impala, convertible, vintage 1961. The grille grins evilly, a hungry shark grin, and the fins splay out behind, so I can see their wing tips around the intervening body of the car, sleek and sexual, metal amphibian. They were not my dreams. The car is a block away now and aims at me. I cannot see the driver.

My friend Helen, whose dreams they were, is dead. She has been dead for years. My heartbeat flutters and a knell of pain rings in my knee. The car approaches but does not reach me. Helen foretold her own death, she died in a white Impala convertible, vintage 1961. She was the only person I ever knew who had the second sight, the gift of telling. It was a burden to her. She sought her death. For years, she dated only men who drove white convertibles made by Chevrolet. The name is a sleek beast, African and swift. I close my eyes again, and when I open them, the car is still there, like a stuck slide in the carousel, persisting between clicks. I think I have inherited her dream. I think the car will kill me if it can.

But I am strong, a runner, and too sensible for the fear that's settling on me. I shake my head, to banish it, edge closer to the parked cars that line the street, this quiet street of sleepy trees and birdsong. In my world of children and floorwax, of duty and plain white underwear, there are no killer Chevrolets. Dead friends do not come back. The car passes me, just inches from my hip, my rib cage, and I wipe away the sweat that's gathered on the crest of my eyebrows, resisting the impulse to turn and watch the car recede.

I cough. I laugh. The street is empty of people and of cars. A squirrel, dusty and city-wise, darts across the street in front of me and claws its way up the bark of an elm tree. There are old leaves in the street, oil stains on the pavement, patches of dried mud that look like sunlight against the gray cement. I'm sweating freely, metabolizing last night's wine; I imagine yesterday's poisons evaporating from the surface of my skin. I lift my knees higher and feel the pull in my thighs, approaching the corner where my course turns left. The cars herded at the stoplight are usual: a Volkswagen, a Pontiac, a plumber's van.

My daughter is four years old now and does not like me to run. When I get up and put on my shorts, my blue shoes and athletic socks, she asks me where I'm going, and when I tell her, she begs me not to go. She watches as I bend and stretch and blow, getting ready. Don't go, Mama. I laugh. I go. Her face is grave, framed in a door pane three feet off the ground. I smile, wave at her and run away. She will be there, watching, when I return.

I hear a car behind me and automatically veer left, toward the curb, even though there is no oncoming traffic to necessitate a squeeze. The car downshifts, a malevolent rumble, and for a moment I feel hot engine breath against the backs of my legs. The shallow vee of white metal wings appears in front of me, the silver letters: C H E V R O L E T. MJR 892. I chant the license number again and again, until it merges with my breathing and the cycle of my shoes. Exhaust fumes linger, souring the air.

Helen died of a broken neck. She did not appear to be hurt, but they took her to the hospital anyway, for observation. Her mother came. Helen sat up to greet her and her spinal column snapped in two. That was seventeen years ago. She was the kindest person I ever knew.

When I turn left again, I am face to face with its chrome leer, the squinting headlight eyes. Somehow I am not surprised, not surprised by its same-side wheelie, turning, or the scream of its tires, or the outcry of the shocks. My daughter watches a stretch of empty street, waiting for her mother to appear. Helen would have been a good mother, tender and loving, but she was afraid to pass her gift of self-fulfilling prophecy along. The night she told me how she would die, I held her and she cried. I never doubted for a moment that she knew.

I take to the sidewalk, where I will be safer. The white Impala, having hung a U-turn, drives beside me, slow as my own pace, an escort. I front-focus my eyes and do not look at it. The engine hums, lazy and guttural. I feel it as a kind of caress. I was three thousand miles away and hadn't seen Helen for several months, but I knew when the call came she was dead. I thought maybe if I didn't answer the telephone, it wouldn't be true, that I could hold death in abeyance, but the phone kept ringing, ringing.

"She was riding in a white Impala," her mother said. It made me cold. I stayed cold all that winter. I learned to run.

I am proud of the steadiness of my gait, the strength of my ankles. I watch my blue shoes devour the sidewalk. I am locked into a stride that lands on cracks, but I do not think my mother's back will break. Abandoning my route, I cut across a corner lawn, but the white car seems to anticipate the move, accelerates and turns with me. It becomes a right-side presence and begins to feel familiar there. The real impala, namesake beast, is not a predator. Helen was almost saintly, too good to live. Often, confronted with a moral choice, I wonder what she would have done. I know that if I do not try to run too fast, I can keep running for a long time.

Perhaps the white car will run out of gas. I picture something sharp, a nail or shard of glass, puncturing its tire, axle or fan belt breaking, the carburetor coughing to a halt. Perhaps the battery will die. What else can go wrong with cars? The Impala is twenty-two years old. Perhaps it will swerve into a tavern and buy itself a beer.

I am getting tired, my muscles glow with fatigue. I wish I had not thought that: Tired. Half a block ahead, an old man, thin and gray, rakes grass clippings from his lawn. I could stop. I could tell him I'm being followed, ask him to call the police. He does not look at me as I draw near him, as I come to a panting halt and jack-knife forward, hands to knees.

"Excuse me. Sir?" I have to touch his arm to make him look at me. When he does, his grin is wide and missing teeth. He points at his big brown ear and shakes his head. Across the street, the white car idles, waiting. Nodding to the old man, I gulp down air and begin to run. The car slips into gear.

Helen was only eighteen when she died. *She died. She died.* My shoes take up the rhythm and pound it out. I was eighteen too and death was alien. Reality cracked for a moment and she disappeared into that fissure. There was no funeral. Her death was an abstraction, a numerical operation. Four billion minus one. *She died. She died.* I was depleted, but not afraid. Now I am thirty-five and my daughter waits at home for me. My lungs are bellows of cracking leather, no longer so firm, so sound as once upon a time.

She died. She died. She died, as my blue shoes remind me. It is useless to try to evade the white convertible. Its canvas top is gray with age and weather, the fancy spoked hub caps dull with mud, there is a deep dent in the driver's side door, but its fins are proud and sensual as ever, its engine is powerful and sound. It knows my route, my neighborhood. There is no turn it cannot take, no median it cannot jump, no alley too narrow for it to pass. The upholstery is red leather, but the interior no longer smells of leather. Inside it smells of dust and sex and Lucky Strikes. Helen admired men who smoked unfiltered cigarettes, who drank hard and drove fast. *She died.*

My muscles ache with a stress no shower will relieve, no liniment will warm away. I have run as far as I can. It is time to run home. By the time I get there, my daughter is grown and my husband is old. I embrace them. Across the street, the white Impala finds a parking place.

The Birch Tree

IT WAS not difficult for my two cousins—boys, friends, and somewhat older than I—to choose their trees the spring our great aunt announced she had a special gift for us. By then we knew our great aunt Faith's gifts were not like the gifts most people gave each other, not at all, but reflected her particular obsessions and represented, perhaps, an attempt to pass those obsessions on to us, her grandnephews and me, her sole grandniece.

Gifts from Faith were likely to be birdfeeders—odd wire mesh appliances that required a weekly trip to the butcher to keep them stocked with suet, or bulbs to grow strange plants from, or funny little books that promised to make the stars, or birds, or weeds our friends. One year in our Christmas stockings we found little white envelopes with what appeared to be five misshapen chick peas inside. Later in the day, at Christmas dinner, Aunt Faith informed us that they were nasturtium seeds, and proposed a kind of contest between the three of us, with an undisclosed prize to be awarded to the most successful gardener among us at summer's end.

Since the boys chose and won almost every game we played, since they teased me unmercifully at family gatherings and were outspoken in their distaste for girls in general, I became determined, that Christmas day, to grow more, *many more*, nasturtiums than they. I could scarcely wait for spring to come so I could plant my five seeds, and persuaded my father to let me take the little plot of soil that ran between the neighbors' red fence and our tiny city backlawn for my garden.

Anyone who has had any experience with nasturtiums knows that they are apt to spread like weeds, proliferate like rabbits. Mine did. They ran amok, challenging the borders between flower bed and lawn, sneaking under the fence into the neighbors' yard, taunting my father's sedate climbing roses with their aggressive behavior. The neighbors did not like nasturtiums and my father took umbrage on behalf of his roses, but win I did, by default, actually, since Phil and Lucas lost their seeds long before the planting season came.

My victory with the nasturtiums led Faith to believe there was more hope for me than for my cousins. The prize was a narrow herbal, already old, with a bright orange cover and tissue-thin pages full of botanical Latin inside. These alternated with thick glossy pages sporting minute and remarkably detailed hand-colored pictures of a variety of plants, salutary and deadly. At six I hadn't much use for the Latin and found the pictures only mildly interesting, and I prized the herbal more for the success it represented than for any intrinsic value I found in it. My enthusiasm, though, led Faith to redouble her conversion efforts, and, that fall she presented me, *only* me, with a season ticket to a series of Audubon Society movies shown Tuesday nights at a local theatre-cum-concert hall.

Tuesday was a school night and the movies, interminably long, started at 8:30— a civilized time for adults, but one to stretch

74

the attentiveness of a first grader almost to the breaking point. Past it, in fact. The narrator had a creamy monotone that lulled me to sleep, and the films themselves lacked the cunning anthropomorphism that Hollywood uses to engage children in real-life adventure. Ten or fifteen minutes after entering the theatre and settling into my plush loge seat, my eyes would grow irresistibly heavy; within half an hour, I would be asleep. Only one film, about the life cycle of fireflies, do I remember at all.

Faith was disappointed in me; I knew it and each week resolved that I would, I *would* stay awake. Each week I fell fast asleep. At last she concluded, wisely, that I was a little too young for the movies and began to reinforce any expression of interest in the natural world by other means.

When I painstakingly planted a little dish garden for the school flower show, she gave me small, delicately carved bird figures to nestle in among the pickabacks. She told me about the plaintive cry of the nighthawk, and how hard it was to sight. This captured my imagination, and I spent countless summer dusks sitting on our city stoop, listening for the nighthawk above the traffic noises from a nearby thoroughfare, and fantasizing every passing pigeon into that lonely, romantic bird. I convinced myself, and believe it still, that I sometimes heard the nighthawk, but the memory I have of a dark, graceful bird-shape swooping across the past-sunset horizon I am sure is only a dream.

But this is the story of our trees, and that story begins on the Easter Sunday of my seventh year, with the family, my father's, or the eccentric side, convened at Faith's for dinner. The day was brisk and bright with the pastel sun of spring and Treetops, Faith's house, almost relieved from its winter exposure by fragile fresh leaves on the trees surrounding it. Before dinner my cousins Phil and Lucas and I were consigned to the finished room in the basement to play. Play! For me it was more like torture. With no adults to fend for me, I was wholly at the mercy of my cousins, who lost no opportunity to punch or poke at me, or to send little word-missiles, cruelly aimed, that wounded far deeper than I ever let them know.

The long awaited call to dinner finally came and we ran upstairs— me last, of course— to take our places at the long dining table. Before family dinners, we said grace, even though Faith surely was no Christian, regarding Easter more as a fertility festival, I think, than as a religious holiday, and none of our families was given to such piety. It was a family joke of sorts that it was wise to pray before eating at Faith's table, because many of the spices she used she grew herself and the mushrooms she collected wild.

Faith was old then, very old, her eyesight failing, and everyone was, or pretended to be, afraid of being poisoned through some mycological mistake. It is true that I never saw my father praying with such sincerity elsewhere, and I remember a certain hesitation before people began eating, each unwilling to dig in until someone else ate and failed to drop dead. On this Easter, trying to show Faith I appreciated her attention and efforts in my behalf, I bravely attacked my plate and stuffed a heaping forkful of mushroom stuffing into my mouth. When it was clear I was going to survive, my more timid relations began eating, too.

Great Aunt Faith sat at the head of her table looking more than ever like a sparrow, with a small bun nesting in her billow of gray-white hair, her eyes small and very bright on either side of her fine-boned beakish nose. Her expressions and movements were quick and delicate. My grandmother, with larger bones, a greater helping of flesh on them and eyes hollowed from age and reading, sometimes reminded me of an owl, but Faith in her exquisitely drab gray or brown dresses, small, deft and exact, was another species of bird altogether.

Grandma, born pragmatic, scoffed at Faith's love for birds, for trees, flowers and insects, at her choice to live in retirement more among them than with people and found her sister, in a family proud of its eccentricities, the most dangerously eccentric of all. (Perhaps, after all, it was only because when Grandpa died—this long before my time—she expected Faith to take her into Treetops. The invitation never came, and Grandma was forced to live with us, instead. The two were never quite at peace with each other, and never quite at war.)

Between dinner and dessert, Faith drew her brittle little body up to its fullest height and waited, her head cocked slightly to one side, for a pause in the pandemonious conversation of our intensely verbal family long enough to allow her to seize the floor. In this family of ours, one is either very aggressive, or very silent. For the most part, Faith preferred silence, but this day she managed to sneak her reedlike voice into a gap in the bellowing and command our attention. She paused just long enough to give her words the weight of negative space, not long enough to let anyone wrest the floor from her.

"I have decided," she said, "to give the children a very special gift."

Once again, she used silence to good effect, while my cousins and I sat straighter and listened hard. She addressed us.

"I am going to give you each a tree. Of your own choosing. After lunch we will walk through the ravine and you can each choose which tree you want to be yours."

My grandmother could not bear the ensuing silence. She exploded into it.

"Faith, you get crazier as you get older. A tree, for god's sake."

My mother, who came late to the family and never lost the tact she brought with her, said: "What an unusual gift. How did you ever think of it?"

77

"A *tree*?" said my cousins, almost in unison.

"There's no room for another tree in our yard," my uncle muttered. "You expect me to spend a Saturday afternoon moving a goddamn tree?"

"The trees will stay here," Faith said, with a good deal of dignity. "The children may visit them whenever they wish. I hope they will come to regard their trees as friends, and see them in all their seasons."

For some thirty years, Faith had been a grade school teacher, and even though her years of retirement had by now almost piled up to equal those spent in the schoolroom, her voice could, on occasion, recapture the impregnable authority the voices of teachers have.

In the pause that followed, I said "Thank you" from my odd chair at the far end of the table. I too usually chose silence to battle in those days, rarely speaking out to the assembled family; and this, coupled with the unaccustomed quiet that surrounded my words, made everyone take notice and look around.

I blushed under the collective gaze, then saw out of the corner of my eye my aunt nudge my cousin.

"Thank you, Faith," Phil chimed, and only seconds later Lucas said, "Yeah. Thanks."

Having said what she had to say, Faith relinquished the floor and the conversation of the family swelled up again. As it swirled around me, I thought about trees. I did not know much about them, really; to me, a city child, they were an undifferentiated class of being. Of course I could recognize a tree when I saw one— of that I was confident, but as to picking a good tree, a worthy tree to be my very own, that I was not sure I could do. And I was some- what unsure that I would know how to treat a tree that was my own. Perhaps it would not like being my tree.

I hoped that Faith, in her wisdom, had resolved this question, had thought the whole thing through, taking my limitations into account. My cousins did not seem to share my anxiety, but were carrying on a conversation of their own, punctuated by friendly cuffs and kicks, inside the conversation of the adults. Secretly I hoped they would not show me up in the business of tree selection.

When we were through with dessert I helped Faith clear the table, glad to do it for the escape it provided from the table. In the kitchen, Faith talked to herself and to me as we bustled companionably about the business of repairing the wreckage occasioned by dining *en famille.* I brought her plates, platters, bowls, and while she emptied them into containers and stored them in her ancient refrigerator, I rinsed the empty dishes clean as I could and stacked them in the deep porcelain sink.

Once she called me to the pantry window, cautioning me to move slowly, and pointed out a squirrel crossing the branch of a tall tree that reached up from the bottom of the ravine, toward the window ledge. With slow rhythmic movements Faith opened the window, then took some seeds from a brown paper sack and handed them to me. She greeted the squirrel in soothing tones as he put his front paws on the ledge, a little tentatively because of my presence.

"This is my grandniece, Squirrel. She will not hurt you. She is going to feed you today."

Hind legs followed front and the squirrel sat upright on the ledge, tail erect, regarding us.

"Put the seeds in front of him," Faith said to me in the same steady, hypnotic tone. "Easy. Don't move too fast."

I advanced my hand slowly, slowly as I could and placed the seeds before the squirrel. A few stuck to my palm but Faith said to let them be.

"Now back," she said. "Don't come too close."

Cautiously I withdrew my hand. We stood back and watched while the squirrel, with good mannered celerity, consumed his meal. Faith didn't move, and neither did I. When he had retrieved every last seed, he turned and chattered at us in tones that sounded angry to me but must, in squirrel, have expressed gratitude.

"You're welcome, friend," Faith said softly, and waited until he turned away and crossed his branch bridge back to the tree to close the window behind him. I watched his tail flash through the green until it disappeared. Faith handed me the paper sack and I brushed my palm clean inside it. Then we returned to our chores without another word. I wanted to talk about the squirrel, ask questions about him, but somehow sensed that what I had just observed was a mystery, to be experienced and not discussed.

When we were through in the kitchen, Faith told my cousins and me to put on our jackets and come with her. In single file we descended the wooden stairs that dropped at an improbably sharp angle from the back porch down into the ravine. Even my cousins clutched the splintery hand rail and watched their feet closely, going down. Winter had loosened a few of the steps and Faith, going first, warned us of them.

"Theo, I'll have to persuade your father to come around some Sunday and help me make a few repairs," she said. As a young man, my father had been her favorite nephew, and they had travelled together to the 1932 Olympics in Los Angeles where his college roommate was running the half-mile, with Faith footing most, if not all of the bill. They retained a special fondness for each other, never articulated, but perceptible as an undercurrent, as patterns of affection in our family tend to be. For his part, though he thought his aunt half crazy, my father rather admired Faith for her independence and the strength of her somewhat extraordinary convictions.

80

At last we reached the foot of those treacherous stairs and found ourselves among Faith's trees. She was surefooted in her sensible oxfords, despite her age, and led us through the maze of trunks on paths of her own creation. Glad to be outside, the boys chattered and rough-housed behind Faith's back. In last place I walked slowly, studying trees with all my concentration and beginning, for the first time, to see the differences between them. Faith led us around for a long time without speaking. Then she stopped, rather suddenly, and turned to face us.

"Well, she asked, "do you have any idea which trees you will choose?"

Lucas and Phil, caught in a wrestler's embrace, separated and looked at their shoes. I had been looking at trees for the first time, seeing new things and virtues in all, but was far from coveting any particular tree.

"Take your time, then," Faith said. "Look around. I'll wait here."

She sat down on a large rock, close to the color of her shapeless woolen coat. The boys headed off in one direction, I in another. As I wandered through the trees, over the soft mulch of last fall's leaves, it became more and more clear to me I had no idea of how to choose a tree. Should I choose the largest I could find? Was size a virtue in trees? I didn't know. Or should I se- lect the prettiest among them? The most uncommon? A slender young birch caught my eye and pleased it. It was slight and short among the thick dark trunks of fir and pine. It could not raise its head above their years of growth, looked positively puny beside the reddish bulk of the exotic madronas, childish next to maple and oak. That it could stand with such dignity, such serenity nonetheless made me like it, and the afternoon sun filtering through the ceiling of evergreens far above danced on its new leaves and made them shine like something precious and rare.

Still, the birch *was* puny compared to most of the other trees and I was afraid that by choosing it, I would open myself up to ridicule from my cousins. If I could choose any tree that grew in the ravine, surely I should choose an impressive one, big and strong. I heard the boys return to Faith and went back myself. They had found their trees. I followed as they led Faith to the spot.

"There," Lucas cried, pointing at two enormous firs that stood quite a distance apart, but whose long lush branches reached out, high above us, to touch.

"Those trees are friends," Phil said. "See, they're shaking hands."

"And me and Phil are friends," Lucas went on. "So we choose them."

Faith nodded. "Do you know what kind of trees they are, boys?"

"Uh, they're evergreens," Phil said.

"That's right. They're fir trees, and fir trees are evergreen." She nodded again. "A very nice selection. I'll give you a book to read about firs when we get back to the house. They're very interesting trees."

My heart was sinking when she turned to me. The firs *were* very big and very beautiful. And the fact that they were friends and that the boys had solved the problem so neatly and won Faith's praise made me feel lonely and inadequate. I think Faith saw my dismay.

"You stay here, boys, and start getting acquainted with your trees while Theo and I take a little walk."

She took my hand and led me back the way I had travelled alone. "Have you made up your mind?"

"No," I half-lied. "It's hard."

"Yes." She began to tell me the names of the trees we passed. I felt as if I might cry.

"That one's very pretty," I said, a little doubtfully, pointing at a madrona.

"Yes, it is," Faith said. "Do you want that to be your tree?"

I hesitated and stared at the madrona, wishing I could say yes with a certain heart, but something in the madrona seemed foreign to me, and some loyalty for the little birch tree tugged at me.

"No? I didn't think so."

We wandered on, repeating a similar exchange about several other trees. Once we came in sight of the birch, my eyes kept turning toward it, but I said nothing and tried hard to find another tree I could want even half as much for my own. Finally Faith led me gently in the direction of the birch tree.

"You know, Theo," she said, "I would have expected you to choose the birch tree straightaway. It's always reminded me of you, somehow. And it's a fine tree. One of my favorites. It's young now, so you could watch it grow up, right along with you."

My heart overflowed and so did my eyes. I threw my arms around Faith and hugged her tightly with a rush of grateful love. Then I hugged my birch tree, too, and laid my cheek against its satiny white bark. As I had anticipated, the boys did make fun of me for my choice, but Faith told them there were some things they didn't understand, and I didn't care what they thought anymore, anyway.

In the year that followed I visited my birch tree as often as I could persuade my father to visit Treetops with me. A few times I even spent the night or a whole weekend there, crawling into bed next to Faith in her long flannel nightgowns and was delighted to learn some of her secrets, like that she let her hair down from its bun at night and brushed and braided it. I fed the squirrel many more times, and came to recognize some of the birds that visited her feeders and sang to her.

My birch tree grew perceptibly. I watched its leaves get larger and darker through the summer and begin to change color when autumn came. It almost broke my heart when they shrivelled before the November wind and were shaken loose from their places, dry and dead.

I collected handfuls of them in a paper sack and kept them in my desk. Faith assured me the birch didn't mind its winter nakedness, and that I could look forward to the pleasure of seeing it bud again, come spring. She was right, of course. The new leaves were every bit as lovely as the old had been, and she convinced me that it was a good thing to learn to let go without regret, and to welcome changes, because they came whether you wanted them to or not. Trees knew that, she said, though people often forgot.

Her illness came suddenly, in midsummer, and struck hard. Faith suffered a stroke that left her partly paralyzed, and she had to be put in a home, a 'guest house' it was called, because my mother couldn't find any practical nurses willing to tackle the tall stairs at Treetops, or to live alone with an old woman on the edge of a ravine. Her mind began to let go and wander of its own accord. She talked of people long dead and of things that had happened many years before, when she was young. Sometimes she would sit in her chair for hours, the nurses said, and make bird calls, animal sounds. They thought it very strange, and called her, among themselves, the 'bird-lady.' But she always knew me when I came to visit her.

Except the last time. It was at the Thanksgiving holiday, and even though they knew the end was very near, my parents gambled on Faith living until we returned from a four day trip to Canada, my first and, planned partly, I think, to ease the fact that there would be no family Thanksgiving at Treetops that year. We stopped at the guest house to see Faith the night we left town. The light was dim in her small room and she did not open her eyes. Her white hospital gown exposed more of her flesh than I had ever seen, so I could see how little of it there was stretched over her small bones. Her face was thin and sharp and she looked, on the big white pillow, as though a strong wind would blow her away like the leaves.

The doctor arrived while we were there and my parents stepped outside the door to talk with him. I stayed by Faith, saying her name softly, hoping I could rouse her from this untimely sleep. Once she moved her head slightly to one side, and my pulse raced; I was sure she would open her eyes and talk to me at any minute.

She never did. We had a nice time in Canada. On Sunday night when we arrived home, Faith was dead. She had never re-gained consciousness.

As was her wish, she was cremated and a memorial service was held for her a few weeks later. My mother bought me a hat for the service, and the organ music made me cry, even though my father said there was no reason to be sad: Faith had a long life without too much suffering at the end.

Treetops had been empty through summer and fall. The relatives wanted to sell it, and my father proposed to spend a Saturday there, getting the house in shape to be shown to prospective buyers, starting to sort out Faith's things. I had not been there since early summer, and asked if I might go with him.

"Sure," he said. "I'd like the company. It's a spooky old place. It won't make you sad, will it?"

"I don't think so," I told him.

We let ourselves in the back door with the skeleton key that Faith hid under the eaves. The house *was* spooky without Faith in it, knowing she was dead. A thick coating of dust covered all the dark furniture, and I saw dust particles circling inside the shafts of cold December sunlight that pierced the yellow shades. While my father dusted furniture, swept, and started to pack up books and other possessions, I wandered through the house, remembering things that had happened in each room. A mouse jumped out of a dresser drawer and gave my father a terrible scare. I stood for a long time in the pantry, planning to feed the squirrel if he should come, but he never did.

We went out for lunch, and spent a long time over it. After the mouse, my father was none too eager to continue his explorations.

"I feel like a graverobber," he explained, "going through her drawers."

At last we ran out of excuses to linger and went back. Before we went in, I said to my father, "I think I'll go visit my tree."

"That's a good idea."

"Daddy, do you suppose whoever buys Treetops will let me come see my tree sometimes?"

"I don't know," he said. "If they seem like nice people, we could ask them."

I went down the old steps alone and ran to visit my birch tree, but I couldn't find it, and grew angry with myself for forgetting so soon. I took bearings by the rock where Faith sat the day we chose our trees and tried to retrace our steps from there. Maybe the winter light was playing tricks on me. I walked concentric circles, getting bigger and bigger, but did not find my tree. I recognized the surrounding madronas and pines, could see almost precisely where my birch tree should have stood. To make sure I was not going crazy, I crossed the ravine and found my cousins' trees. They still stood holding hands.

A strange kind of panic overcame me and I ran up the stairs to find my father.

"Daddy, my tree's gone."

"You mean you can't find it," he corrected. "It's been awhile since you were here."

86

"I *know* where it's supposed to be," I told him. "And it's not there."

My father stood up and brushed the dust from his hands. "Let's go see," he said.

I led him to the spot where the birch tree should have been, and we both walked all around looking for it. He put his hands on my shoulders when we returned to the empty spot.

"You know, Theo," he said, "The house has been empty a long time. I bet people have been coming down here to cut wood. Birch logs burn very well. Someone has cut your tree down for firewood, I'm afraid."

I got down on my knees and began to dig through the dead, drifted leaves.

"What are you doing?" my father asked.

"Looking for a stump. There isn't any stump. If someone cut down my tree, there'd have to be a stump."

"So there would," said my father. "So there would."

But we never found one.

The Copper Mine

ALONE AT last, Roger drew the newest still-unsavored *Playboy* from its hiding place deep in a stack of *Consumer Reports, Sports Illustrateds,* and *Atlantic Monthlys* and with deliberate fingers found the stapled center of the magazine. There might or might not be articles on either side of center provocative enough to excuse his having bought it; he'd check the table of contents later, but for the moment he wasn't interested in writers or their bylines. Right now it was the bottom line, the topless, bottomless, hairless, flawless, honey-lighted, expertly airbrushed, lip-parted, long-thighed naked female centerfold he wanted to peruse. Obligingly, as if anticipating his need, the magazine fell open. And Roger froze.

Eyes ashine with invitation, lips pouted pinkly, his daughter's face stared back at him. He looked below the face. The model had enormous breasts. Even though Roger rarely studied his daughter's body anymore, even though to look at her body at all these days made him uneasy, he knew his daughter's breasts weren't half that size. It wasn't her.

And yet the model's hair was the same color, cut the same way. Her eyes were sea green, too, her nose described the same imperious curve. She had high cheekbones and green kneesocks. Perched on the naked model's nose were precisely the same slightly overlarge hornrims his daughter wore to study or to watch TV. His eyes dropped lower, followed the pale curve of a hip to the very center of the centerfold, then quickly looked away. He hadn't seen his daughter *there* since she was toilet trained.

Even though the model was not his daughter, the resemblance had the impact of a thousand cold showers on him. The warm tingle he'd felt opening the magazine was gone, perhaps forever, and his flesh felt sad. The naked model was not a day over eighteen. Roger was fifty-four and he knew he would never buy a copy of *Playboy* again.

Somehow, he blamed his daughter.

They engaged in a long French kiss, sloppy and playful. Curt's teeth felt and tasted different from her teeth, and Theo liked this. She liked his curious, pointed tongue. His hand nestled under her T-shirt, his fingers teased her skin, and she liked this too.

Suddenly, the porch light came on. Seconds later, it blinked off and thereafter— on, off— continued the alternation. Inside the dark shell of Curt's DeSoto, eyes closed to make a deeper darkness, Theo could feel the flashing of the light against her lids. She retrieved her tongue and whispered, "My father."

Curt pulled away. "I'd better take you in."

Theo felt abandoned, cold where Curt's hands had lately touched her. "Ignore him," she said. "Kiss me instead."

But Curt didn't feel like kissing her under paternal scrutiny.

"Let's talk, then," she said, setting her hair straight with her fingers, tucking her T-shirt in.

"What do you want to talk about?" Curt asked.

"I don't care. Anything."

"Your dad must be very protective."

"Not really."

"That's a pretty ingenious signal you've got worked out."

"It's unilateral. After eighteen years, he discovered last week that I'm alive. All in all, I wish he'd forget it."

"Aren't you being kind of hard on him?" Curt asked. He seemed uncomfortable, to have found a hard edge in her softness.

"I don't think so," Theo said.

"What's he been doing for the last eighteen years?"

"His own thing," Theo said.

"Let's do it," Roger said. "Let's do it this summer before you go away."

Theo laughed, then looked closer at her father. "You're kidding, aren't you?"

"No," Roger said. "Why would I kid you? Besides, I promised."

"When I was six, you promised we'd go when I was twelve. I'm eighteen now."

"I know," Roger said. "It's probably our last chance. You want to go or not?"

Her voice was neutral, the rise of her shoulder said she didn't much care, but Roger thought he saw a flicker of pleasure in his daughter's blue-green eyes. "Sure, Dad. Why not?"

After so many postponements, she found it hard to believe they would really take the hike, but her father's enthusiasm did not abate. He got a map and found the trail on it, dug out his backpack and when he saw it was mildewed and moth-eaten beyond use, bought two new ones at an Army surplus store. He aired the sleeping bags, washed the nesting aluminum pots and pans, found sterno for the little cookstove, took her to Penney's to buy them each a pair of workboots and heavy socks for hiking.

"We'd better get in shape," her father said, and every afternoon for two weeks, they put on their new workboots, to break them in, and walked for several miles on the flat city streets. As they walked, her father pointed out things along the way— a kind of storm window he'd never seen before, a woman with a figure like a fire hydrant, or asked her a steady stream of small impersonal questions, which she answered tersely, yes or no.

Theo almost enjoyed it, except when young men in cars passed by and gave them speculative looks. Then she felt embarrassed, not because they would think she was walking with her father, but because they might think the man she was walking with was not her father. He was still vigorous and attractive, and she thought it was possible that a young woman who was not his daughter might walk with him.

Sometimes older drivers stared at them, too, and once her father chuckled and said, "Look, he's jealous."

After the first set of blisters healed, her feet and the workboots accommodated to each other. Every day, they walked a little farther.

Roger lay in bed and listened to the rain. After a dozen years of promises, they were going to hike to the copper mine and it was going to rain. He tried to remember the trail and the first time he climbed, a footsure boy scout with good wind, but the picture he conjured up had himself in it, and that made the memory unreliable. The smell of evergreens in rain (did it rain then, too?), the fickle smoke of a campfire corkscrewing in the wind, a crazy momentum of descent he remembered but could not be sure of their source. There had been many trails.

Roger resisted the impulse to light another cigarette and for a moment listened to the eccentricities of his wife's breathing. Curled away from him, she gurgled and sighed. Roger began to breathe deeply, stretching his lungs. It was a long time since he had thought about breathing.

In her sleep, his wife shifted a knee and rolled from hip to stomach. The change silenced her wheeze briefly, until all the obstructions and reservations shifted, too, and she began to snore again.

For all she could remember of her childhood, she'd wanted to make this trip with her father, yet when he woke her before dawn on the appointed day, Theo felt angry. The bed was warm and for once her dream was going well. In it, she had been about to make love for the first time with a Curt who was not really Curt, but more handsome, more tender. Her father's hand felt cold on her shoulder, and she scowled up at him in the uncertain morning light.

"Rise and shine," he said.

Theo groaned. As her senses woke up, too, she heard the weather. "It's raining."

"I know," her father said. "Good thing we waterproofed our boots."

It was a long drive, more than two hours, into the forest where the trail began. A hard rain pelted the car and there was no dawn, only a slow lightening of the sky from gray to white. The tires hissed, slicing through water. His daughter sat as far away from him as it was possible to sit in the same car and kept her arms folded close across her stomach. Roger thought about the postures of women, of his wife curved away from him in sleep, and how they could shut men out without a word.

He liked the diner where they stopped to eat, a small box of yellow light inside the rain, smelling of coffee and sausages and wet wool; he liked the worn men with brown hands bent over big breakfasts and their necessary silence. One big-hipped, lank-haired waitress mothered them all, and Roger liked the chevrons of smile lines that veed out from her eyes, he liked the thick carrot shape of her legs and her implacable morning cheer. His daughter's face, across from him, seemed blankly young.

Roger wanted her to like the greasy potatoes and the limp bacon and the quiet wind-browned loggers, too, but he had no way of telling if she did. Her silence was different from the men's silence, and when the waitress came around to fill their coffee cups again, his daughter muttered thanks without looking up. Would it be different, Roger wondered, if she had been his son?

It stopped raining. They helped each other on with their packs, and Theo waited while her father leaned against the car and smoked a last cigarette.

The trail was wide at first, corrugated Cat tracks melting into mud that sucked at their boots. They walked abreast and the air smelled of wet earth. The toes of her yellow boots turned brown with mud, and she was glad they no longer looked so new.

This is what it's like, she thought. It was not like she imagined at six. Crows scolded them for coming. After half a mile, they reached a large open space where two Cats, a bulldozer and a backhoe stood like grazing dinosaurs. The torn earth around them was the same new yellow-brown as her boots and bled a dark brown mineral ooze. Upended trees crisscrossed the landing, their root wads muddy and ornate. The bulldozed earth seemed more indecent to her than the pictures of naked women in the magazines her father hid and she sometimes found, than her own dreams of sex. She wondered if the rawness offended him,

94

too, but could think of no way to ask him that wouldn't sound foolish said out loud.

Beyond the clearing, the trail entered the forest and no machine tracks marred it. Its surface was paved with fallen needles. Occasionally, a crotchet of exposed roots crossed the path, and at first, feeling light-footed, she leapt across these, but her father said, "You have to save your energy," and after that, she stepped across them, as he did. They still walked side by side and as they walked, their strides lengthened and loosened and fell into a common rhythm.

Roger felt good. Two hours out, and the slope was still gentle. Memory must have exaggerated the pitch of the trail. The sun burned through the morning mist, until the air felt dry and the woods around them were patched with sunlight. Whatever made conversation so hard at home or in the car eased up a little and they talked when the trail or the woods provided topics— a cluster of early mushrooms, no-see-ums swarming (they didn't sting), the seedy sweetness of wild blackberries, bracket fungi grown like pale shelves on the trunks of trees. Not big subjects, certainly, not the ineffable wisdoms he'd lately felt such pressure to impart, but he liked naming things for her, and she seemed to like it that he knew their names.

Once her foot slipped and she scraped her elbow against a tree trunk, stopping the fall. It was a small hurt and she made light of it. Roger looked into the woods. He found a Balm O'Gilead and laid its healing leaves on the abrasion. "I learned that in Boy Scouts," he told her.

His daughter smiled at him. Her face was pink and sweaty and no longer seemed so characterlessly young.

By midday, they were hungry. They shed their packs in a small

95

clearing and let the breeze dry the wet backs of their shirts. Her father leaned against a tree trunk and smoked a cigarette while Theo found running water and filled a pot from the August-shallow stream. The sandwiches she'd made the night before tasted much better than she expected, and it felt like playing house, having everything they needed so neatly packed, the raisins here, the chocolate there, nothing extraneous or out of place.

"Let's rest a while," her father said. He used the pack for a pillow and spread his jacket under his shoulders, then lay back with his hands crossed over his stomach. He closed his eyes.

For a moment she didn't know what to do. For once her father didn't want to talk. She swallowed the words that had been slowly bubbling up and walked around the clearing, found the damp black remains of an old fire, then found the largest patch of sunlight and lay down in it. The sun was warm on her skin and red behind her eyelids and the pleasure she felt puzzled her.

Usually when her life did not progress in its own context, she felt as if she were waiting, outside of time, and did not like the feeling, but she was not impatient now. Someday she would camp in the woods with her lover, Curt or someone else she didn't know yet, but today she was hiking with her father. Today two birds she couldn't see trilled to each other in the treetops and a small stone she was too lazy to move pressed against her thigh. Her father napped with his canvas hat covering his face, his denimed legs spread and the toes of his boots pointing out. She had a strong sense of his otherness. A breeze stroked the soft hairs on her face and arms. She dozed.

Roger's lips swelled and cracked. Every breath was a coarse file rasping the back of his throat. His pack grew heavier and his head lighter. Blotches of black or red sometimes smeared across his vision, so he could not see the trail. The trail was rough and narrow, mercilessly steep as it tracked the edge of the cliff, and it frightened him not to see it clearly. He could feel his heart at work inside his rib cage and the flutters of pulse at several distinct points around his body. Sweat rolled down his forehead and clung for a moment to his eyebrows before it fell into his eyes.

Spending precious breath, he called out to his daughter, twenty yards ahead and climbing. "Let's stop for a little while."

Her legs stopped their steady churning and she turned to look at him. "We stopped ten minutes ago."

"I know," he said. "I'm sorry."

He was less sorry for her than for himself. She bounded down the trail to him, not caring that she gave up ground.

Roger leaned back, letting a rock ledge assume the weight of his pack. His heart slowed, and when its beating no longer dominated his awareness, he looked down at his daughter, crouched beside him on the trail.

"When I was a boy," he said, "I practically ran up this mountain."

His daughter did not seem as surprised as he was that he could no longer sprint uphill. She picked up a stone and threw it over the sheer edge of the trail. Both of them listened for the bottom of its fall.

There was a warmth along her thighs and her muscles felt elastic. Her breathing slowed and deepened until it counterpointed the brisker rhythm of her strides. She imagined the skin that held her shape in space was a thin translucent membrane, permeable by light and air. Colors seemed bright and subtle. She counted greens. In a symphony of treetop birdsong, she could pick out the paired duets, throaty question, cooed reply. The smells of the woods blended a scent she wanted to save and wear forever, as her own perfume.

She had been satisfied, sometimes, with her accomplishments, excited by romance, but it surprised her as she felt and named it that joy was so simple a sensation, and so light.

"Let's stop," her father called, and her brain agreed before her body did. Her legs did not want to stop climbing. It was hard for her father and she was sorry, but she did not want to stop. With effort, she braked her yellow boots.

The peak is not of manhood, but of youth.

The words found each other, sorted themselves out and stuck together. Roger did not at first recognize them as a thought, but took them for another temporary congregation of random syllables. Chanting made climbing easier; if his mind was full of mantra, there was no room left for pain.

The peak is not of manhood, but of youth.

Examining the new refrain, he found that it had meaning, and that its meaning, grasped by his body, made his heart beat even harder, and erratically, it made his dizziness more profound. His atoms danced frantically, threatening to detach themselves from molecules.

But of youth . . .

His daughter was young. He let her climb in front. His maleness gave way before her stamina. She belonged to the trail and bounded up it like a deer or an elk. The rhythmic alternation of her strides animated her hindquarters, and he watched this as form, with no embarrassment. He no longer pitied the thinness of her wrists and neck, but wondered at her strength. He envied it, too, though he supposed it was not seemly to do so.

Not seemly.

Seem to whom? Who wouldn't envy? Any declining animal envies the ascendant. But his daughter. He had never expected to envy her. She climbed. He watched her climb and she was tough

and strong and something else, too, which derived from her fe-
maleness. She was delicate, climbing, and moved over the earth
as if she meant it no harm.

Each of his boots felt as heavy as his pack. He dragged them
uphill, pitting his will to climb against his body's will to stop.
This is the wall that runners talk about, he thought, but he knew
he would not be able to outrun the wall. When his legs refused to
move and his will refused to make them, he called uptrail to her.
"Let's stop. I need a rest."

"Your father is a very strong man," her mother always said, and
when she was little, Theo found this reassuring. *If my father is
strong, then I am safe.*

His voice reached her, calling for rest. When she turned to
answer, she found he had fallen far behind, was lost to sight
beyond the last curve of the trail. She began to descend to him,
and descent felt different from climbing. Her boots thumped the
trail emphatically, and the weight of her pack pushed her to
hurry.

If my father is not strong, then am I safe?

As she rounded the curve she saw him, red-faced and panting,
on the trail below. He bent forward under the weight of his pack
and took ease like an athlete after running. Only they had not
been running. She still breathed through her nose and her skin
was dry except for the hot place under her pack.

If I'm strong, am I safe?

Alerted by the crunch of her boots on the trail, her father
raised his head and waved to her. Theo waved back.

Am I strong?

By the time she reached her father, he was sitting against a
tree and had his feet raised on a fallen log. He looked up at her. "I
must be getting old," he said, and laughed as if it were a joke.

Theo didn't know what to say. Finally she said, "Well, if you are, so am I," although she knew it wasn't true.

Her father patted the ground beside him and she sat down and shared a Hershey bar with him. A rustle drew her attention and she looked up in time to see a red squirrel suspended against the sky, leaping from one tree to the next. The squirrel landed, gripped the swaying branch for a moment, then disappeared among the needles of the fir.

Theo wondered if the squirrel felt safe.

Meeting the ranger gave them an excuse to stop, so Roger was genuinely glad to meet him. The ranger rode a roan horse and led a mule loaded with camping gear on a long rope. He was headed downhill.

"You gave me a start," the ranger said. "I didn't know there was anybody up here. Thought maybe you was a cougar."

"You sounded like the cavalry," Roger said.

The roan horse pawed the trail and sniffed the air. The ranger took off his hat and scratched his head. He looked like a young man but talked like an old one. "Yep. I been clearing out the shelters up ahead. Trail's closed after this weekend." Roger caught him eyeing Theo and tried to think of some way to say she was his daughter. "Up this high," the ranger went on, "you can get early snow."

Roger squinted at the sun above them. "I don't think it's going to snow," he said.

The ranger, too, looked at the sun. "I guess not. Still, I'm glad I know you folks're up here. Where's your car?"

"Parked on the shoulder, heading north, about six miles out of Quilcene," Roger told him. "Blue Ford."

The ranger nodded. "I'll swing by Monday morning and see if she's still there. When you two planning to come down?"

100

"Late tomorrow afternoon," Roger said.

The horse had dropped its head and was nibbling at a stand of grass beside the trail. The ranger tightened his reins, ready to move on. Roger wanted to prolong the rest. He shifted his pack. "Tell me, how far is it yet to the abandoned copper mine? I hiked up there when I was a boy, and I promised my daughter years ago I'd take her in to see it."

The ranger looked uptrail and then turned back to them. "It was about ten miles up ahead, but you're twenty years too late. The shaft collapsed a long time ago. It's grown over so good by now you'd never find it if you didn't know just where it was at."

"Gone," Roger said. He expected it to be changed, but not gone.

The ranger consulted his Timex. "Well, if I'm going to be in time for my supper, I'd best get on." He jerked the horse to attention. "Sorry you won't get to see the mine, miss. I never did either."

Roger and Theo stepped off the trail into the woods to let the ranger pass. He had to tug and shout at the mule to get it moving.

Roger leaned against the broad trunk of a first-growth cedar and studied the armor of woody plates that was its bark. Their pattern seemed both deliberate and inscrutable. He had to tilt his head straight back to see the topmost branches of the tree. Would his daughter blame him that the mine was gone? Slowly, holding to the straight line of the trunk, he brought his gaze back down.

"Well," Roger said, "it has been forty years. Nature can be pretty unforgiving." He looked at his daughter and saw that she was older than he'd thought. She smiled and said, "So much for destinations."

After they met the ranger and their goal was gone, it seemed almost as if her father had gained strength. They climbed two hours more in dogged fits and starts, while the sun moved west

101

until it was too low to penetrate the thickness of the trees. They did not discuss stopping but knew that it was time to stop when they found a wide, flat place where the last rays of the sun still reached. A shallow pit with the charred end of a log in it showed them others had rested here before. They could hear from its flowing there was water nearby.

In silence they unrolled their sleeping bags and spread them out six feet apart. Her father laid down on his back and Theo laid on her stomach and used her forearms for a pillow. Her muscles tightened as they lost warmth and she felt as if a large weight pressed her against the earth. As the sun dropped lower, it grew chilly and Theo thought about crawling inside the sleeping bag and how good it would feel, but she was too tired to make the effort.

His daughter slept. Roger pulled the extra sweater from his pack and laid it over her. He found wood and built a fire. The water in the stream nearby was clear and cold and he drank greedily, slopping on his shirtfront like a child. As dusk settled in, the woods around their little clearing were full of scurrying sounds. Roger knew if he kept moving, his legs would stiffen less.

Light from the fire danced across his daughter's skin, and she slept as she had when she was a baby, with her face turned to one side, lips parted, with a child's mysterious expression, oblivious and deeply concentrated. He did not wake her until the rice was simmering in its pot over the sterno cookstove. Roger saw she didn't know right away where she was or what she woke to. He put his hand lightly on her forehead and told her not to worry, everything was fine.

Her father huddled on one side of the fire, she on the other. Occasionally he stood up and leaned across the fire pit to pass her his flask. The whiskey in it tasted like liquid flame. It sank to her kneecaps and glowed there. Occasionally, she stood up and turned around to warm her backside. Then she could see the ripples of their firelight tickling the woods. It could only touch, not penetrate, and she did not like to think about the darkness beyond the circling shadows. She turned back to the fire and to her father. They seemed to be waiting for something to happen, for something to give them permission to call it a night.

Her father drank from his flask. He lit a cigarette. He coughed. His eyes found hers across the flames. "I suppose your mother has talked to you a lot about ..." He paused. His face was shiny in the firelight. "About sex," her father said.

She nodded. "Yes."

"Your mother is a wonderful woman. I love her," her father said. "And she loves you very much, you know." Across the fire, her father's eyes were almost pleading.

"I love her, too," Theo said, because he seemed to want her to say that. It was true, though not something she thought about a lot.

Her father no longer looked at her, but straight into the fire. "I just wanted you to know," he said, "that it's all right to enjoy sex. It can be very nice. It's supposed to be."

"I know, Dad," Theo said.

Roger lay on his back on the hard ground and stared up at the stars above the clearing. He remembered that when he was a boy, the vastness of the night sky had seemed to hold a kind of promise. Now it simply seemed vast. He closed his eyes on it and slept.

"Well, I'm glad the bears didn't get you," Curt said.

"I was afraid they were going to," she told him. "I stayed awake all night and listened to the noises in the woods. I was afraid that if I went to sleep, bears would come, or wolves, or mountain lions. I was afraid my father would have a heart attack and I'd have to carry him down that steep trail, or that he'd just die in his sleep and I'd be there all alone. The wind came up and howled for hours." Theo laughed. Already the terror of that long night began to fade.

Curt laughed, too. "Sounds great," he said. "Let's get a pizza."

His wife sat on the edge of the bed in her pink robe and spread liniment on the back of Roger's legs. Her touch was gentle, but even so his tender muscles winced. When she was done rubbing and his skin began to sting with heat, Roger turned over onto his back and saw then that his wife was close to tears. He asked her why.

"It's just that sometimes she seems so young. I hate to let her go."

"She'll be alright," Roger said. Somewhat painfully, he sat up and looked at his wife. There was white in her dark hair, even a frost of silver on her eyebrows. Her face was as familiar and as strange to him as his own. He looked in it for signs of the beauty that once dazzled him, and was grateful to find it tamed and dimmed by time. Softly, sadly, he kissed her powder-scented cheek.

The Afternoon of the Poetess

I AM eleven years old and the poetess is wearing dark glasses in the tearoom.

"How absurd," she says, handling the chunky silverplate with pleasure, reveling in her finger sandwiches. She laughs at the tearoom and loves it. She does not know how closely I watch her. She does not know that I, disguised like a pork chop in blue frills, am studying to be a poetess, too. She does not see herself beneath my baby fat.

"Next year," she tells my friend, her daughter. "You can shave your legs next year. You're still a child."

I shave my legs now. It is a privilege that came with my first period. Elizabeth does not have her period yet, longs for it, as did we all before our bodies mysteriously deposited that first triumphant stain in our flowered cotton underpants.

"Theo shaves her legs," Elizabeth says.

The poetess glares at me. I decide to change the subject. "Why do you wear sunglasses inside?" I ask her. I truly want to know, feeling that the sunglasses are somehow close to the source of her magic, but she thinks I am being impertinent.

"What's wrong with wearing sunglasses inside?" She punctuates the question with a carrot curl. "If you must know, I can't bear for people to see my eyes. It makes me feel so vulnerable." She inserts the carrot between her red lips, snaps it in two with her impressive teeth. I return to my sandwich.

"Evelyn," Elizabeth says, "Mrs. Fogarty didn't like that poem I handed in last week." Elizabeth by fiat must not call the poetess "mother." The poetess refuses to be defined in terms of Elizabeth's existence. I have seen her slap Elizabeth for slipping.

"The woman is a horse's ass. It was a fine poem. At least after Richard and I touched it up a bit."

Mrs. Fogarty didn't like my poem either, but I wrote it all myself. I have envied Elizabeth's poem all week, feeling its superiority to my own, and am delighted to learn it was not entirely her creation. Our teacher *is* a horse's ass. I like the expression, as I like others I have learned from the poetess. Her words are quickly incorporated into my working vocabulary, until Elizabeth says, "oh, you sound just like my mother," and my own mother says "where in heaven's name did you pick up that sailors' talk?"

An ancient waitress removes our raided plates, replacing them with lavish sundaes crowned with whipping cream, dripping with nuts— chocolate for Elizabeth and me, butterscotch for the poetess who cannot bear to be prosaic.

She looks at her watch. "I have an appointment in the designer shop in half an hour," she says. "We'll have time to stop by the book department first." She licks vestigial butterscotch from her spoon like a cat. I am a glutton with my sundae, cool and sticky-sweet, finishing before Elizabeth. The waistband of my blue skirt strains, incising me, and I wish I were tall like the poetess, skinny like her daughter. When I picture myself a poetess, I am long and small, far from my present self. Somehow I will be so when the time is ripe; I live now for the person I will become.

The waitress brings the check. I reach for the folded dollars my mother has given me, but the poetess waves them aside and pays with her metal charge-a-plate. She signs her name boldly, making the biggest capital letters I have ever seen. I wait for the waitress to recognize the name, but she merely nods thanks for the gratuity and spirits coins and autograph away. The poetess pushes back her chair and smiles at the ribbons and flowers atop the heads of other patrons as we thread our way out of the tearoom.

She enters the book department grandly, always a step or two ahead of Elizabeth and me, who bob like refuse in her wake. Her eyes absorb and dismiss the two tables of new arrivals, Scylla and Charybdis of the book department in this department store.

We go to the darkly paneled shelves along the west wall, where the books show their spines, as they do in the library, instead of their faces. A neatly lettered sign reads *"Belles lettres."* I have often pondered the sign on my solitary pilgrimages here, translating it over and over in my sixth grade French, but knowing that it means "beautiful letters" still does not tell me what it means, and I have finally been forced to decide there must exist a school of literature I have not encountered yet.

Here the poetess looks for her newest book, and I wonder to whom she has written. Maybe to the poet who is often just coming or going from her room when Elizabeth and I get home from school. He is pleasant enough, sometimes eats cookies with us in the kitchen and never seems to mind that the poetess is usually still in her nightgown when he arrives. I have not imagined him a writer of letters, and it is hard to know what they have left for letters when they talk so endlessly.

"Only three copies," the poetess observes, running an index finger lightly over three slender dusty-pink spines that have her name on them. They are on the top shelf: I strain to see them.

"Oh Christ," she says. "What ignominy. They've put me next to Rudyard Kipling. You're a better man than I am, Gunga Din."

A clerk who seems more than a clerk in his pinstriped suit and shining shoes approaches us, palms together.

"You were looking for something? Perhaps some poems for the young ladies. We have an excellent selection of children's verse along the opposite wall."

The poetess turns the panes of her sunglasses upon him and he falls back a little. "Walter de la Mare," she intones. "Lewis Carroll. A.A. Milne." She pauses. "Yecch. I hardly want my daughter to waste her time with that palaver. Actually," another pause, "I was checking to see how my latest book is doing." She pulls one from the shelf. Her photograph is on the back— minus the dark glass, a good likeness.

"Of course, Miss Kittredge. I didn't recognize you at first. It must have been your glasses. Of course. A lovely book. Your best to date, if I may be permitted an opinion. We've already sold at least half of our stock." The clerk backs away a bit more. "And it is, it is a real privilege to have a writer of your stature living in our city. Just the other day I was saying to Mr. Mason— he's our manager— that we should perhaps consider a small autograph party in honor of your new book. You have so many admirers locally."

"Have your Mr. Mason call me then," the poetess says.

"I will. I will." The clerk withdraws.

The poetess turns back to the shelves and picks out a black and white volume considerably bigger than her own. She turns it in her hand. "Dear Dylan," she muses. "What a tragic waste." She does not reshelve the book but lays it on the counter. I read the name over my shoulder as we leave, resolving to look for it in the library.

We are more cordially welcomed in the designer shop. A woman with rhinestones on her glasses who seems to carry a medicine ball inside the bodice of her black dress greets the poetess enthusiastically.

"Right on time, Miss Kittredge. Wait till you see what I've got for you." Dandruff falls to her shoulders from her hive of hair as the woman leads us to a room walled in mirrors. The room is as big as my bedroom. The poetess puts a Camel in her cigarette holder and lights it with her silver lighter while the woman carries in an armload of dresses and hangs them on hooks around the room. The poetess follows her circle, studying the dresses.

"The gray wool is interesting," she says. "No. I hate that shade of green. It makes me look malarial." The green does not get hung.

"This one you'll like," the woman says. "It's worn like a sari."

The poetess begins to undress. I do not know where to direct my eyes. She doesn't wear a slip, only a sturdy brassiere and stockings that turn into underpants and show a dark prodigious thatch of pubic hair. The poetess is large but not fat. I learn that she wears a size fourteen.

She plucks at the yards of paisley cloth on the hanger. 'How the hell do you get this on?"

"Wrap around. I'll show you. You'll want to take your bra off for the right effect." The woman unhooks the poetess' brassiere and takes it from her.

The poetess' breasts fill the room, staring at me with huge red-nipple eyes from every mirrored wall. There is nowhere I can hide my eyes from their amazing gaze. I have seen only my mother's breasts before; my own are new, only beginning to be breasts, only a little ripple of flesh across my recently flat breastbone, only a subtle curvature that seems to me uncommonly sweet and secret.

But the poetess' breasts are a commanding presence. It is as hard for me to imagine flesh so deep, so defiant on a woman's body as it is to imagine having whiskers sprouting from my smooth face as men do. And it is even more exciting than whiskers. I know that I will masturbate when I am home tonight, remembering this. I am eleven years old and do not know the word, but I have recently discovered the process, squeezing my legs together until a feeling flowers between them. My body knows what it knows.

The woman wraps the paisley around the poetess, leaving her shoulders bare, and steps back to consider the effect. 'Or," she says, "you can wear it on one shoulder."

The poetess looks in the mirror. She pulls the drape further down, exposing one breast, cyclopean. "Now this would create quite a stir," she says, turning slowly to study herself from all sides. "Roman matrons used to bare their bosoms at dinner parties, I've heard."

The woman laughs.

"What's to prevent me from going to the fabric department and doing this myself?"

"The label, dear," the woman says sweetly.

I still stare avidly at the poetess' breasts. They flash before me until she juggles them unconcernedly back into the sturdy cotton casing of her brassiere.

The clerk turns to Elizabeth and me with a smile of stifling sweetness, "Did you like that one, girls?" She talks down to us, voice lilting and simple.

Elizabeth nods no, not especially. She is digging in her

mother's purse. The woman does not expect an answer from me, but turns to help the poetess shimmy into an endless gown of gray wool. She slides the zipper like a caress up the poetess' back. The dress looks to me as if someone has made over one of my father's suits. It is severe and mannish. When my mother wears evening gowns they are made from satin or brocade. They remind me of princesses in fairy tales, of butterfly wings.

The poetess is delighted with the gray dress. Its neckline stretches straight across her collarbone. Her amazing breasts retreat into its gray folds. "With my turquoise jewelry, I think," the poetess says. She has forgotten us. Her fragmented self absorbs her, dancing in the mirrors. I cannot decide which poetess to watch, there are so many images of her around me.

"I'll take them both," she tells the woman. "Charge." She pulls on her black sweater and tweed skirt while the woman takes the dresses lovingly in her arms and retreats. The poetess sits on one of the white iron chairs.

"Get me a cigarette," she tells her daughter. Elizabeth takes the holder from the ashtray and removes that last forgotten stub from it. She inserts a fresh one from a silver case and gives it to her mother.

"That's good," the poetess says. "I won't have to worry about clothes for a while now. What do you think of them?"

I am too cautious to venture an opinion on things I don't understand, and I do not understand the dresses. I am trying to think of something original to say. Elizabeth holds up a plastic case.

"What's this, Evelyn?"

The poetess stiffens in her chair, leans forward. Elizabeth opens the case and removes a peculiar object whose utility it is impossible to guess. It is a circle made of something firm, with a soft, transparent, rubbery filling. The rubber does not fit the circle tightly, but makes a shallow cup. My aunt has a portable drinking cup for taking pills that opens like a telescope, and I conclude that this is a variation of the same device, less pretty than my aunt's, which has colored jewels on the case.

"Put that away. Right now." There is tension in the poetess' voice. Elizabeth hears it too, and has heard it too often before not to know that unless obeyed the voice means trouble. Slowly she replaces the thing in its case. The woman returns and gives the poetess a slip to sign.

"Send them, please."

"Of course."

"What is it, Evelyn?"

"Shut up," the poetess says. "I'll tell you. It's called a diaphragm. And it's to make damn sure I don't have any more accidents. Like you."

Elizabeth and I are eleven years old and do not understand the accidents of adults, but we are silent as we follow the poetess to the parking lot and do not look at each other.

At the museum the poetess pays my way again, not out of charity, but without thinking of it. My purse is heavy with my mother's unused dollar bills. A large crowd has gathered for the exhibition and we have to wait in line to go inside. This is the first day of the show and we are there to see it. The poetess has seen it already, two nights before, at the opening.

She shepherds us like small dogs toward the main gallery and we half-run to keep up with her, so our footsteps echo in the marble vestibule. I am suddenly afraid. My own mother takes me to tearooms, buys dresses, but this world is new and I feel like an alien in it, conspicuous as if I had just stepped off the boat at Ellis Island dressed in somber rags. I straighten myself and try to seem serene.

The poetess nods at the museum guard sunk on his too-small

chair. I close my eyes entering the gallery, afraid I will not be able to understand or even maybe, as with the emperor's new clothes, I will not be able to see at all. When I open my eyes, they are assaulted by colors. As we advance, the colors sort themselves into discrete shapes of pictures on the walls.

The lights are very bright. I have expected silence, reverence, as we are made to observe on our yearly school trips to the museum, but conversation flows around us like water, rising and falling, spraying us unexpectedly when it hits hidden rocks and erupts into laughter. At first I cannot believe these clustered people speak my native language, they are so easy in the presence of art. I feel they must belong to a species different from my own. Wholly awed, I am silent in the wake of the poetess.

Her voice joins the others as she picks a canvas in midgallery where the crowd is thin. Our tour begins. I should be listening to what she says, learning what she knows, but I cannot separate her voice from the others. There is a strange tight feeling behind my eyes; I strain like a runner waiting for the start of a race. I expect something great of this, some lasting revelation that will shape my life, much as I did a year ago, before I had decided to grow up to be a poetess and expected to feel the holy ghost invade me when the bishop laid his hands on my head to confirm me. I felt nothing, except the bishop's musty old man's breath impinging on my nose. I do not want to be disappointed again.

The canvas is enormous, a jumble of colors and shapes that make no sense to me. I tackle it taxonomically, making myself observe and describe it in minute detail. If I miss a single subtlety, I am afraid the whole will be lost, the classification faulty. Elizabeth looks bored, exercising with royal grace her child's right to boredom. I envy her passivity. I have never worked so hard.

After a while I am exhausted. My brain can sort and catalog

no more. We stop before an all-white picture. Paint peaks and swirls from its flat pristine surface like mountains that pierce the clouds when you are flying above them, looking down. At last something touches me— a song without words, a poem that does not need to be written to be known and loved. My tired senses rest in the white valleys.

I am sure of myself now. Excited. "I like it," I say, and it is a brave, a dangerous thing to say.

The poetess laughs. "Henry is such a showoff. *Epater la bourgeoisie.* I bet he broke a jar of mayonnaise on the kitchen floor and couldn't bear to waste it."

I am puzzled by this punishment. Blood rises under my skin and beats in my ears. I want to retract my words and more, to deny my spontaneous rush of approbation. I follow the poetess closely, listening to her comments, unworthy to feel until I know what she feels. Because she is at home here, because Elizabeth is openly fidgeting and I am inconsequential, she does not bother to verbalize or defend her opinions. Her face, her hands, the low tones of her voice serve as my guides. Now I catalog those as carefully as the colors and forms before.

A man with a camera strapped to his back enters the gallery. Another man by his side carries a variety of wired apparatus, a microphone in his hand. A big white '5' is painted on his camera.

"Well, well," the poetess says. "The world must have been asleep today if they're coming here for news."

The cameraman pirouettes slowly to pan the gallery. The microphone man approaches a conversational knot and unties it with his questions. The poetess pats her hair and pretends to be unaware of them. She turns away from the camera and approaches a picture that makes us stand in profile to the camera. The poetess begins to tell Elizabeth and me about the painting, in more detail and in a louder voice than she has discussed any of

114

the others. She points to areas of the canvas with silver-ringed fingers. Elizabeth ignores her, stares boldly at the newsmen. The flow of conversation around us has gained momentum since their arrival; from a stream it has swollen to a river. I follow the poetess' lead, though she does not notice me, playing rapt student to her instructor. We circle gracefully to the next canvas as though we dance together to a shadow tune that no one else can hear. Elizabeth mars our minuet by straggling unevenly between us.

"And here's one of the lights of our local art community," the man says to his microphone. "Miss Evelyn Kittredge, the poetess."

The poetess pivots smoothly to face the camera, her face all surprise, drawn out of deep concentration.

"Why hello, Charles. I thought I saw you come in."

"Enjoying the exhibit, Miss Kittredge?"

"Oh yes. I think it's so important to know what's going on in our corner of the world. As I was saying to my friend Richard Davis at the opening Thursday night, I believe that every year this show gets stronger, more impressive."

"Are those young ladies with you?"

"Yes, Charles, they are. This is my daughter Elizabeth." She touches Elizabeth's shoulder fondly, turning her toward the camera. The man with the microphone stoops toward her.

"You're lucky to have a mother so well equipped to expose you to the arts. How do you like the exhibition so far?"

"It's all right." Elizabeth points her fine face, perfectly bored, at the camera. Coming out of his avuncular crouch, the microphone man spots me.

"Oh," the poetess says, "and this is Elizabeth's friend, from Miss Wright's."

"What's your name?" the man asks, and I tell him my name with all the dignity I can muster with the blood rushing in my head this way. When my tight cool voice reaches him, he is surprised and looks at me for the first time. I think perhaps he recognizes, as the poetess does not, the poetess hidden in my frills. Amazing talent. What precocity. Such promise. I fantasize, staring into the mesh web of his microphone.

"Why don't you show us your favorite painting, young lady? And tell us why you like it."

I look up at the unexpressive panes of the poetess' dark glasses. The cameraman makes ready to follow where I lead. For a second I think about the man who has made the all-white picture, with its monochromatic mountains, its purity. But only for a second. I walk by his picture, its whiteness only a flash at the edges of my eyes. I lead the man to the large canvas where our tour began. The poetess would not have started our tour there if it were not good. I begin to tell the man my observations of the painting I have studied so painstakingly. I tell him why I like it. The microphone darts and shines in front of me. I am eleven years old and will be a poetess myself someday.

Defoliation

WE STARE at ourselves in the long glass panel in the door of Jonathan's apartment house, coming out of the rain together, a couple. We are borrowing Jonathan's apartment tonight because we intend, for reasons obscure and personal, to unvirgin ourselves. We are going to Do It at last, I because I am leaving soon, want desperately to come back to this boy/man, and know that I never will. I want to give him something that I will never give to anyone else in the years ahead of me, when he thinks we will be together and I know already we will not.

Why he has chosen to give me this particular gift I do not know, except that he is a man, must unburden himself of it sometime, that he hopes, perhaps, it will make me come back to him. Jonathan is in the kitchen waiting for us, his dinner eaten, dishes in the sink. Although he knows, more or less, what tonight portends, he is too cool, too kind to make reference to it. Jonathan is twenty-four, a failed philosopher, and in love with one of my friends who, like me, is only seventeen, pretty and fickle. I suspect that something pleases Jonathan in the impossibility of loving her. Jonathan is the kind of person who thrives on sighs; he has recently become a Catholic.

Jonathan's apartment is nice, in the ways that our parents' homes are not. It is old, for one thing, and retains the smell of his dinner. There is a bearskin rug in the livingroom in front of an incapacitated gas fireplace, red bulbs in the old wall sconces, and an elaborate tape deck featured as the altar is in the furnishing of a church. One whole wall is devoted to the storage of books, mostly religion, philosophy, and mysticism, and of tapes, mostly classical and flamenco guitar.

We have a drink together. Jonathan is in no hurry to leave his kitchen for the rainy night outside and we are in no hurry to have him go.

"When are you leaving, Jill?" he asks me.

"Ten days," I tell him. Curt bolts his drink.

"Excited?" Jonathan asks.

I make a noncommittal noise. Of course I am excited; I have been waiting for this for seventeen of my seventeen years, but I do not want to say so in front of Curt. Jonathan the Romantic puts an arm around Curt's shoulders.

"Cheer up, man. It isn't long till Christmas. We can stay drunk in the meantime."

"Long enough," Curt says. He makes himself and Jonathan another drink.

"Think of all the love letters you can write," Jonathan says. "You can revive a lost art form. No one writes good letters anymore. And you can save them to show your children. Jill can tie them up in lavender ribbons and keep them under her handkerchiefs."

"I don't use handkerchiefs, Jonathan. Kleenex has made handkerchiefs obsolete."

118

"Underpants, then," Jonathan says. He and I laugh. Curt has finished his second drink already and does not laugh. I look from his long, shadowy face to Jonathan's delicate one. Someday probably I will love men with faces like Jonathan's, but tonight I love Curt with his large bones, his big eyes—familiar square-jawed Curt. Loving him now as he sits getting drunk at Jonathan's kitchen table, I feel a rush of not wanting to go, am almost willing to scuttle seventeen years' planning to escape for him.

Curt drinks from the bottle now and Jonathan stays on. I take the bottle from Curt and make myself another drink. Running the water over Jonathan's dishes, I offer to wash them.

"It's the least we can do," I say.

Jonathan sits down at the table with Curt while I fill the sink with water and suds. The smell of the detergent washes the air clean of dinner smells and I am rather sorry to part with them. Curt and Jonathan are talking in the yellow kitchen light. I cannot hear what they are saying over the running of the rinse water and the clatter of plates, but I am strangely happy inside this little capsule of time, of things happening and sounding and smelling and looking just this way in the yellow light of Jonathan's kitchen. The dishwater has steamed the rain-chill from my fingertips and I know that if things could stay always precisely like this, I would never go away.

But there are only so many dishes, soon enough washed, and only so many excuses for Jonathan to linger on with us. Before he takes leave, he shows Curt how to operate the tape deck. I fold the dish towel over the back of a chair. Jonathan puts on his jacket and carries his umbrella to the door. Curt and I follow him like a couple bidding their last guest goodnight, only Jonathan says "I'll be home around twelve-thirty, one, I guess," and we remember it is his house and not our own. Curt locks the door behind him; we return to the kitchen and I pick up my unfinished second drink. I raise it to Curt in a toast and he, leaning against the gas stove, raises the scotch bottle back at me. Glass touches glass.

"To us," I say.

"Yeah. To us," Curt says. He tips back his head and belts straight from the bottle. When he rights it, I see for the first time how much of it is gone. Curt staggers a little against the stove. I take the bottle from his hand, put it on the table, then put my hand in his.

"Come on. Let's go in the living room." I drag him along. A guitarist picks his heart out, unseen by us; courtesy of Jonathan, music fills the room. As soon as I curl my feet up under me on one end of the sofa Curt, who has been sitting close, moves a little. I can think of nothing to say to him for the moment and he evidently has nothing to say to me. This is a moment I have conjured up in fantasy a hundred times at least; the setting is right, details in place, the red light shines, but this awkward silence has never been in my scenario. Somehow we are not, for the moment, conspirators, perhaps not even friends.

The fear in my heart is my own fear, female fear. This is the night of my defloration, my initiation, my First Time. This night and no other. Somehow I am under incredible pressure to take in every detail, register every sensation, separate and savor every note of the music swirling around us, see into every shadow the red light makes. I see the worn spots on the bearskin rug, and the long white teeth of the bear fixed in a permanent snarl in his still jaw.

Everything is familiar now but Curt's face, which has become a stranger's face. I realize suddenly that he is afraid too, and that his fear is probably not like mine. If we touch each other, I decide, once we touch each other, everything will be all right. But for awhile I cannot touch him; I think about touching him and cannot move the body that houses my thoughts.

At last he moves toward me a little and puts his hand on my knee. I start a little when he touches me, then lean into his shoulder and absorb his warmth. His palm is damp on my knee. We kiss once, awkwardly, then more and longer until kissing feels right and good again. My mouth and chin are wet. We kiss and kiss.

Curt is alternately gentle and rough. My body, my skin begin to light up with touching and my mind gets quieter and quieter inside, words replaced by quick, dark images. When I open my eyes, the room swims in the red light. Curt breathes rapidly. His skin grows moist under my fingertips and his beard rasps my chin a little even though I know he has shaved specially tonight.

We perform the ritual we have performed so many times, whenever and wherever time and place and absence of other people have permitted, but never consummated. Incantation by response, we proceed. We have become naked and my fear is translated into excitement, becomes excitement. The moment, my moment, comes nearer and nearer.

Curt stands and pulls me to my feet, toward the worn bearpelt on the floor. The cool air encases my body now it is no longer touching his.

"Wait," I tell him. "Let me take my tampax out. I'll be right back."

I go to Jonathan's bathroom and squat on the toilet. The tampax string is slippery with excitement; I pull it out and flush it down. Before I go back to the livingroom, I take a quick look in the mirror, seeing myself between the streaks of Jonathan's shaving cream.

"This is it," I tell my blazing eyes. My chest is mottled red and white and my face is bright pink.

Curt is posed awkwardly on the bearskin when I return with a towel— an overgrown baby waiting for the photographer to come take pictures that will always be an embarrassment. I spread the towel on the bear and sit on it. We have chosen this time because it seems impossible to become pregnant when menstruating, and we do not want to become pregnant. Curt's naked back curves toward me. I lean against it, pressing my breasts against him.

"I love you," I tell him. My declaration goes unanswered. When he turns toward me I see that his erection is gone; I have been away too long. I rise up on my knees and kiss him, then he lies down with me. We climb again, undulating on Jonathan's bearskin rug until I am more excited than I have ever been.

For the first time in months, I do not think of going or of coming back; for the first time in my life, I think of nothing at all. I perceive without words, and what I perceive is Curt's face, his dark eyes and slightly fleshy lips. My blood yells "ready." Metaphors of fulfillment flash behind my eyes.

He climbs between my legs and tries to enter me, a woman, for the first time. I want to know how it feels. The mechanics I leave to him. He pushes and shoves, bumps against me, feels me with his fingers, but does not enter me. He swears and mutters while my nerves stretch tighter.

"Help me," he says finally, between clenched teeth. I try to help, to guide him in, but he is only half-stiff and I do not know exactly what I'm doing. We struggle for a long time and I keep thinking that any second it's going to work, hoping it will, but it never does. Handled and harried, he falls completely, limp as a dead thing. We have no illusions left. He rolls off me, turns away, and does not touch or speak to me.

My skin prickles as the sweat dries on it; my pulse slows down and my naked shoulders grow cold with rainy-night chill. It becomes clear to me that my defloration has been indefinitely postponed. The metaphors are still just metaphors. For awhile I

122

try to think of something to say to Curt, who seems so silent and so far away and who must be so ashamed. I am still looking for something to say when instead of saying anything, I start to cry, a little trickle at first, rolling out the corners of my eyes and down the sides of my face. The trickle turns into a stream, falling silently and steadily, until my ears are overflowing with tears.

I lift a finger to empty my ears, and something breaks inside me. Choking on it, I begin to sob out loud, big, ugly sobs. Curt's back cringes at the sound of them, the skin seems to contract. My selfishness disgusts me; I imagine every sob is a knife leaving a bloody trail in his soft white unmoving body. I know I should stop crying and comfort him; I should be wise and say wise things, convince him I don't mind. I should stop crying and be kind to Curt who loves me and will lose me, but I can't, because I am not crying for what has just happened.

I am crying for everything that has happened in the past, and will happen in the future. I am crying for everyone I ever loved who has died. I am crying for my parents who love each other so unwisely and so well. I am crying because in ten days I am going places I have never been and because if I ever do come home again, neither it nor I will be the same. I am crying because when Curt makes love for the first time it will not be to me, and I am jealous. I am crying for the betrayals of all the men who will betray me, and for the pain of all the men I will betray. I am crying because my parents will die someday. I am crying because I will die someday.

I am crying because my friend will hurt Jonathan. I am crying because all women ultimately will hurt Jonathan. I am crying for all the sad movies I will ever see, and all the sad books I will ever read, and all the music I will ever hear so beautiful that it moves me to tears. I am crying because no matter how much of the world I manage to see, there will always be so much I have not seen. I am crying because I cannot stop crying and hurting Curt this way.

I make an enormous effort to pull myself together and gradually the sobs soften and finally die. My head begins to pound, sharp hammers at my temples. Curt's shoulder looks so soft and round I put my hand on it.

"Curt, I'm sorry," I say. "Jesus, I'm sorry."

He is inert under my hand.

"Listen Curt," I say too late. "I love you. I really do."

Still he does not move. I spend a long time muttering phrases of love and apology at his unmoving back, my head aching as though armies marched through it, gooseflesh rising on my naked arms and legs.

When Curt speaks at last it is to say, "Put on your clothes. We'd better go."

Glad for something to do, I stand up and collect my clothes from where they fell in previous haste. I pile them on the sofa and begin to dress. My clothes have been hollow so long they are even colder than my skin. Curt gets up and retrieves his scattered clothing, stepping into it heavily and always careful to keep his face hidden from me. He fastens his belt and turns off the tape deck, then glances at me quickly and tells me to comb my hair.

I retreat into the bathroom. My face is dead white now, with red spots like wounds on top of the cheekbones. I throw water on my face, comb my hair, stuff a wad of toilet paper in my underpants to staunch the menstrual flow, and do not want to leave the bathroom, ever. In Jonathan's medicine cabinet I find aspirin and take three with tap water to stop the pounding in my head. When I leave the bathroom Curt is pouring the rest of the scotch down the sink.

"Ready?" he asks.

"Yes."

124

We turn out the red lights. I pick up the spotted towel.

"What are we going to do with this?"

"Bring it," Curt says. I fold it up to hide most of the bloodstains and put it under my arm.

It is still raining outside. The streets shine black with it and we run to the car. Curt lets me in, I let him in from inside. I sit against the far door and wait for him to say something, anything to me. He drives in silence, and I try to reach around the pain in my head to the place where words are formed. Several times I start to say things, but my sentences shatter before they reach Curt. He is driving too fast and pays no attention to the center line, dodging the mass of other cars as though he'd like to die. I realize that I would not like to die and ask him to slow down.

When he pulls into a park near my parents' house I think that we will talk now, but he drives the car up to a trash barrel and tells me to throw the towel away. I run out in the rain and stuff the bloody towel into the garbage can.

"We'll have to get Jonathan a new one," I say when I get back inside. He does not start the car immediately, so I ask him if he wants to talk. Apparently he does not want to talk.

"You do know that I love you, don't you? At least tell me that. I love you, Curt. I really do."

He at least tells me that, nodding wearily. "I know."

I realize with horror that he says it to be kind, letting me believe he believes what is not true. I wonder how long he has known and has been kind to me like this. He knows as well as I do that when I go it will be for good. There is nothing I can do with the guilt or with the love I suddenly feel so I, like he, look to the world beyond the next ten days, when we will be in different places forever, and keep my mouth shut as he drives me home.

Story for Susan

WRITE A novel about a model going to Hollywood, you said, and your name will be a household word. You will be rich.

Your suggestion, Susan, makes me nervous. So well used to poverty, so comfortable inside it, I fear the disruption of riches. The smell of money is the smell of sulphur. I can't help it; the precepts of discarded Christianity and of my newer if diffuse socialism combine to insist that "rich" and "immoral" are synonymous. And as much or more than wealth, I fear fame. Unfamous, I'm vulnerable enough. Still, I want to please you, to requite your long investment. A model goes to Hollywood.

It rings familiar; as myth, I know the trip—an American shorthand for the pursuit of dreams. Played one way, it's a fairy story; turn it around, and you have a cautionary tale. Though no one in America does or is supposed to live happily ever after. We love Howard Hughes for his misery. Our morality is vigilantly middle-class, even if our fantasies are not. Wealth corrupts and

127

beauty fades. Watch a few hours of television, any night. You'll see.

Our model, presumably, wishes to exploit beauty to obtain wealth. I'm trying to summon everything I know about models, and it's damn little. Once when I was thirteen, a fancy kids' boutique invited me to model their line of *Chubette Fashions* on a local afternoon TV show. I was chosen for being the least unattractive fat adolescent available at the time, not truly fat but merely, well, stubby, still within help of the long waists and vertical stripes the makers of *Chubette Fashions* produced as palliatives for the overweight.

I know you think of me as a thin person, but this is not true. In my dreams, I am fat still; my self-image is fat. Once fat, always. It seems odd now to think I would let my excess weight be exploited publicly, but remember, it was 1962, in the long gap between suffrage and liberation, and to be on television for whatever reason was something like the secular equivalent of a religious experience. To reward my services, the proprietors of the Fairy Frock Shoppe gave me sixty percent off the price of a white sharkskin coat-dress that was indeed "slimming" and also inappropriately dressy for any occasion in my fat young life. It yellowed in my closet long after my fat was gone.

I assume you would like my model to be thin. Although it might be refreshing to make her both very beautiful and very fat, a sort of evangelist for the possibility of being both at the same time. Has there ever been a great fat heroine? Is there market research to suggest how she would fare? I'm trying to envision, from my city days, the body type of subway readers. Endos or ectos? I imagine for the hefty reader (they must be numerous, to make the diet books the staple of so many publishers' lists) there's satisfaction in vicariously experiencing life as thin through literature, though perhaps it would be canny to take a chance on an obese Jane Eyre. We might even have a cult book on our hands.

Actually, I'm probably not ready for that myself, having just figured that what's kept me from quitting smoking for so long is a fear, morbid, and, I hope, unfounded, of getting fat again. Our model will be gloriously, lissomely thin, though with a generous bosom for her sylph-like form to support. Thus do we impinge on fantasy; genetic accident produces only four or five such women per century, I think, unaided by Maidenform or silicone. Let her be one.

She comes, since all of us who don't reside in New York or Los Angeles are provincial, from the provinces and is, as most of us these days, impoverished and wanting not to be. She comes by bus. It is below zero in Cleveland when she boards the Greyhound wrapped in her form-obscuring winter coat. Someone near her on the bus has a thermos full of kidney stew, the pervasive odor of which makes our model gag every time the thermos is opened. She is not fond of viscera.

Next to her on the bus sits either 1) a garrulous aging prostitute, or 2) a wild-eyed young religious fanatic on his way to join a world-renouncing commune. Perhaps both. The whore, a generous and expansive soul, rather short-sighted, so that her makeup is not only garish but slightly off the mark, offers her lovely seatmate, our heroine, some sage advice. Don't end up like me, she counsels. Don't sell yourself too cheap. Men's always lookin for a bargain where they don't deserve it.

The young man, on the other hand, might identify his own normal and healthy libido, enflamed as our heroine removes first her coat and then her heavy sweater as the bus grows warmer, as the tenancy of an external devil who tempts and tortures him. Night falls outside the tinted windows, the steady road song of the bus wheels lulls our heroine into a gentle sleep. Her fair head droops toward her chest, the overhead reading lamp illumines the fineness of her skin and casts the spiny shadow of eyelashes on cheek below. The young man watches obsessively and cannot bear her beauty. He is an aesthete who is trying to be ascetic. His own proclivity for passion undoes him, and in religion he seeks a turbid numbness he mistakes for grace. The temptation he suffers watching her sleep is dreadful. He wants to touch her so badly it makes him ache, both locally and ecumenically.

Sometime during the night of trial, he denies the evil in himself and projects it onto her. He envisions her as the whore of Babylon, as Salome with his own head emplattered, as weak Eve in the Garden, citizen of the Wicked Cities, traitoress to God and righteousness. She wakes to his denunciation, vehement and incoherent, her big innocent blue eyes blink sleepily, startled by his rage. This makes him madder still. He's screaming now, raises his hand to strike the temptress down. A black man in the aisle seat across the way grabs the upraised arm and stops the blow from falling. The driver stops the bus in the emergency lane and comes back to see what's going on.

Our model huddles terrified against the window, while the prospective monk inveighs against her. All her life, she will remember the fast, mad, rubbery working of his lips around the big, archaic words of denunciation, the spittle bubbling at the corner of his mouth, occasionally spraying her.

"He just went crazy, man," the black passenger volunteers. "He'd been starin at her all night, and then he started screamin."

"Has he hurt you, miss?" the bus driver, a stocky middle-aged fellow with a grizzled crew cut, an ebullient tattoo concealed beneath his uniform shirt, solicitously inquires.

"Oh, no," she responds uncertainly. "No, he just frightened me."

"Well, enough of that" The driver grabs the fanatic's shoulder.

"You're coming up with me. Next stop I put you off."

The fit past and passion cooled, the young man drops his head with submission reminiscent of early Christian martyrs in the movie version of *Quo Vadis*. "His will be done." The driver prods him up the dark aisle. The fellow across the way pulls out a flask and offers our heroine a snort. "Make you feel better. Help you get back to sleep."

She smiles and shakes her head. "No thank you. I don't drink."

The black man shrugs, swigs from the flask, recaps it and returns it to its hiding place. He reaches up to extinguish his reading light and reclines in the dark, his long legs contorted in the short space between his seat and the back of the next. Our heroine leans over and turns off her companion's still-burning lamp, then retreats to her window seat and stares out at the dark, at the passing flicker of house and street and car lights the bus approaches and quickly leaves behind.

She's pensive now, stunned by the seemingly unmotivated attack she's just endured. It's a good time for reverie, a time to rub elbows with the past. Caught in night, when motion is elusive, she thinks of what she's left behind—all she *can* think about, since what's ahead is unrevealed, a little frightening—and home thoughts offer solace. She thinks fondly of the kindly, mildly eccentric maiden aunt who raised her.

An orphan, she is, which allows her to exist outside of sociology and beyond reach of Freud. Most of literature's best heroines, and many of its heroes, have been foundlings. In the British and European traditions this was, I suppose, a neat way to cut one's protagonist loose from the heavy anchor of class, to set her free on the tides of adventure, fate's vessel. Or perhaps unparented is something we all secretly wish to be, free of the guilt, the responsibility and love inherent in being someone's child, never to face those troublesome moments of truth when we see we are balding just as our fathers did, or hear ourselves remonstrating with our children in our mothers' voices.

Great Aunt Winnie is a charming relic, a gentle recluse much concerned about the various species of wildlife she coaxes to and succors in her small suburban home. I suppose I'll have to consult the appropriate Peterson field guide to find out just what kinds of birds habituate Aunt Winnie's feeders. At any rate, her great-niece's dream of a career in Hollywood seems no more or less probable to Aunt Winnie, no more certain of attainment or less worthy of success than her own hope of saving whooping cranes from extinction or, with an annual five dollar contribution, of stopping the slaughter of baby seals in Newfoundland. These are the things Aunt Winnie cares about; she is happy enough for her ward to have ambitions of her own. If she becomes rich and famous, our heroine resolves, chasing peripatetic dawn across the continent, she will show her gratitude by establishing Aunt Winnie in a small rural farmhouse where the birds will visit freely.

There comes the moment, of course, when the bus draws near Los Angeles, when eternal summer pursued is summer found. Unseasonably hot, near eighty degrees, the great sprawling metropolis is swaddled in brown, eye-stinging smog. Stagnant clouds hang over the city and obscure the skyline. Our heroine wonders if there are any birds.

Are there? Beats me. If so, they must be mutants, adapted to survival in an ambience of noxious gases. Time now for my second confession of inadequacy: I know next to nothing about Hollywood, was only there once— it was a job, you should know, you sent me— and I was too busy taking care of business to observe the natives or to look for tarnish on the tinsel. I saw no movie stars, only a pride of rich midwestern wives on Rodeo Drive, wearing mink on a steamy August morning and looking for places to spend their husbands' money. I stayed in a pretentious molded plastic and plaster of Paris hacienda called the Beverly Wilshire Hotel, which I would recommend to no one, not even a fictional villain. I was embarrassed by my tenancy there and burned by the covertly contemptuous glances of chicano maids and bellhops, the eternal accusation of the presumed rich by the certifiably poor.

If I lived in Hollywood, I'd have a lot of trouble with that, just as I did when I lived in New York. In some places, so much misery, so much inequity visibly, audibly, olfactorally abounds it seems indecent not to be miserable oneself; one is morally obliged to be miserable either for cause or empathetically. Survivors, the successful, will blindness and deafen their nervous systems to the shrill incessant cry of the streets, of the only species on earth wronged because it wrongs itself. To enjoy such places, to live rich in them, is to prevail at the expense of others.

I live in a small town now, Susan, because grief and deprivation wear neighbor's faces and are personally remediable. I give a loaf of bread to the family whose food stamps are lost in bureaucratic fuddle, I loan books to the woman whose husband has just died so she'll be a little less lonely late at night. There are ways, however small, to help, however sad or inconvenient, to take one's place in the community of human sorrows. By way of recompense, I get to hold the newborns, to celebrate the victories of my friends.

I will not give her, our heroine, my own disease. She is compassionate, yes, but only to those fate casts directly in her path, whose number is, as she approaches Hollywood from Cleveland, exactly zero. She is able to hear sirens without wondering who suffers, able to see old women with rheumy eyes and rags for shoes without needing to know where and how well they sleep.

She has never read John Donne's sonnet upbraiding death with the universality of dying. She is truly free, this young woman— with the round, deep blue eyes, like my daughter's eyes, with silken hair the color of new straw that, like my daughter's, mysteriously turns red when wet. She is kind, but not indiscriminately so, not kind to the point of pain. She believes in God, perhaps, as I do not, but does not accept the terrible burden of human charity. If she should succeed, and I'm not sure yet that she will, she will not stop to ponder whose failure is the dark side of her ascent.

As she steps off the bus in the station bay, she can feel her pulse in all her body. The hazy sunlight surprises her eyes like a photo flash, recording for all time the moment of disembarkation. The air stinks of diesel fumes; they are visible, wavering ghosts rising in the sun. Her own excitement organizes the cacophony of busses and city and people into a song of greeting. She has arrived at the place of dreams.

She should now, since it is only about eleven in the morning and she is curious and excited and wants to stretch her legs, find a locker in which to stash her cardboard suitcase full of panty hose and cheap cosmetics and walk the streets unburdened. The problem is, I have no idea where in Hollywood the Greyhound stops, and if it does, what street she walks. Well, I can check that later, with Greyhound or in the library. Let her walk now in the Hollywood of imagination, down a doubly broad avenue whose comings are separated from its goings by a park-like strip with tall palm trees, a species of vegetation related to the horsetail fern (genus equisetum), and like it, an odd survivor of Pleistocene times, before trees developed the specialized vascular system they have now. The palm trees look like survivors, their trunks scaly and tough, fibrous, like the hides of elongated pineapples, their heads imperially leafy as the fascia emblazoned on the backs of

134

dimes. They appear impossibly exotic to her, waving their suc-culent, moisture-hoarding fronds against the yellow sky.

No less so seem her fellow strollers, the casually elegant, the stylishly extravagant, not merely dressed but costumed at lofty peaks of fashion so immediate as to be ephemeral. Nothing like it in Cleveland, where her modeling career commenced, where she displayed the cautious seasonal choices of staunchly respectable department stores to tea-room patronesses munching finger sandwiches and pouring tea from heavy, silver-plated pots. Here everyone is thin, is tan and appears to be rich, promenading down the palm-partitioned boulevard, searching the polished boutique windows for tomorrow's style with the avidity of souls thirsting for scripture. Among these walkers, slim, streetwise skaters weave a way, the chung-hiss of their wheels casting an aural spell along the avenue. Their legs are long, tanned, bare below abbre-viated shorts. Our heroine's skin is midwest winter pale. In the translucent mirror of a shop window, she glimpses her own round face, the eyes enormous and deeply dark, reflected against black satin overalls inside.

Even the dogs are thin here, skinny-legged and high-rumped, with pointed muzzles and skulls too small to accommodate much by way of brains. They lead their masters, dog hair suavely coiffed in all colors of a Clairol rainbow. Around their thin necks, collars flash with metal studs or shiny gemstones that just might be real.

One woman, startlingly black-haired, exercises a cat too large and powerful to be domestic. Tawny furred, wearing a red leather collar, the beast consumes the avenue with the sure stride of a predator. Everyone, every lithe body on the boulevard is glam-orous and none is famous. These not-stars dazzle with affluent brilliance and make our model feel a blank spot in the universe, devoid of scintillation. If even ordinary people are beautiful here, if ugly people are elegant and the intelligent comport themselves with panache, what chance does she have?

We domesticate our dreams, Susan, so their attainment seems less improbable; we tell ourselves we have a fifty-fifty chance, one chance in two, but success is not a binary operation. Stepping into reality, our heroine sees how statistically unlikely it is that her name will ever be a household word, how small her gifts seem in the great gift show of southern California. Her stomach sounds a hollow ping. Finally, in Hollywood at last, loneliness besets her. If in that moment a bus appeared with Cleveland spelled out in the front window, she would board immediately, leaving both suitcases and aspirations behind as artifacts of a less sad, less wise self.

No means of retrenchment presents itself. Instead a rampant skater careens into her shoulder from the rear, nearly upending them both. If this were the story I'm supposed to write in pursuit of wealth and fame, the man with whom she collides would be an actor, or maybe a producer's son. He would look into her startled, vulnerable face and see the *je ne sais quoi* that promises stardom. Our heroine would experience a collision with her own fate. Not so. The young man, who is assiduously chewing gum, looks passing daggers at her, curses and skates on. She feels wounded in his wake. In fact a tear or two escapes the corner of her smog–stung eyes, and she searches in her purse for drugstore sunglasses to hide her sadness. For the first time, she understands that risk does not assure victory.

So we arrive at one of those junctures whereat in fiction, something happens to alleviate or deepen the pain, where something turns the plot toward its next destination on the roadmap inside the dreamer's mind. In life, tears do not produce such definitive results; they continue to fall or are stifled and wiped away. The feelings that called them forth persist. We are stuck with our sorrows until time dispels them or we simply become bored enough with the condition of sadness that we cease to be sad. Most of us are blessed with an upper limit of despair, past which our nervous systems turn toward desperate jubilation. Not terribly dramatic, not a process especially useful to the story-teller, but one damn handy for quotidian survival.

The best we can say for our poor heroine, who has the misfortune to live in my story and not someone else's, is that she survives her awkward moment on the promenade, walks on until she encounters a storefront McDonald's franchise among the boutiques and goes in to order herself a tray full of comfort food, the reassuringly familiar double cheeseburger, small fries and chocolate shake that look and taste exactly the same in Cleveland as they do in Hollywood. There, with apologies, we must leave her for the moment. My daughter cries in her bedroom; her nap is done. It's a sunny afternoon, and we'll most likely meander down to the riverfront and feed stale bread to the ducks. "Mama," she calls. Insistently. "MAMA." I go.

The ducks liked the bread, and my daughter liked the ducks. It's nearly twenty-four hours now our heroine has been sitting in McDonald's, consoled by junk food. At least she was out of harm's way. Too much in life is left unresolved, too much important teeters always on the precipice to add to one's life the enduring insecurity of characters in creation. There should be a prayer for them, as there is for sailors, for warriors, for those who govern or travel or suffer loss. God succor and defend all the unfinished souls abandoned in the process of conjuration. Watch over them with your abundant grace. Be patient with them and let no harm befall.

The food eases her hunger and her spirit, restores some courage and some strength. Even if risk does not assure success, it is its major precondition. Risk is independent of result and yet essential. Yes, she sees that now, and once again feels prepared to risk, to carry on in this adventure that is all risk. Maybe the world will seem brighter if she finds herself some refuge to call home. The fat directory in the phone booth yields up the address of the nearest YWCA, a chaste and thrifty choice of domicile, and a call reveals that yes, rooms are available, shared bath.

The bathroom has two sinks, two stalls. It is dingy and clean and smells of disinfectant. Our heroine is brushing her teeth when a bathroom co-tenant enters and appears behind her in the mirror, a plain girl, slightly jowly, her coloring a symphony of timid browns. She says, "Hello. You must be the new girl."

Our heroine spits out toothpaste and rinses her mouth. "I guess I must. Hello."

The plain girl ducks into a stall and closes its partial door. "I'm Barbara Miller. I live in fourteen."

Now we must name our heroine; in the half-imagined communal bathroom, several moments of truth converge. Has our heroine known her own name ere now? Is this not her baptism? For a moment, she is poised between two names— the old-fashioned, serviceable one conferred by her departed parents, and a new name of her own choosing, a name made up expressly to call into being the person she wishes to become. She signed the desk register with her old name: Letitia Bell. Letty Bell. Ding dong. Whom she would like to be is the sumptuously, evocatively named Jennifer Beauchamps, the Jennifer for Jones, Beauchamps after a Cleveland restaurant of unimpeachable cuisine. She likes the foreign resonance. Mademoiselle Beauchamps. A name whose owner's hands should be kissed with passionate politesse, a name for the marquee, for boldface captions below wire service photos, for handsome men to whisper over glasses of expensive wine, among the petals of roses.

"I'm Letty," Letty/Jennifer says, "but I want to change my

name to Jennifer. What do you think?"

"You want to be an actress," Barbara Miller observes, and her voice sounds as if she knows everything there is to know about Lettys who wish to be Jennifers. She emerges from the stall. "Don't you?"

"Well, yes. I know it's not easy, but..."

"I'm a secretary," Barbara Miller says. "I'm a very good secretary. I make very good money and have a secure future. You're very pretty."

Letty/Jennifer flushes, her cheeks suffuse with color.

"I'm glad I'm not pretty." Barbara Miller washes her hands with Borax-O from the bullet-shaped dispenser. "If I was pretty, I'd want to be an actress, too."

"What's wrong with that?"

"Only that it never happens. The last three girls I shared this bathroom with wanted to be actresses, too."

"What happened to them?"

"One got married to a truck driver, one got pregnant and had to go home to Oregon."

"What about the third?"

"Cracked up," Barbara Miller says, with something like satisfaction. "They put her away. I went to see her once. After the shock treatment, she wasn't like herself anymore. Not at all. Not pretty either. They made her plain, like me."

"You're not plain," Letty/Jennifer protests. "You have very pretty hair. I bet you'd make a great blonde."

"Think so?" Barbara studies her visage in the mirror above the sink. "But I don't want to be blonde. I don't want to be pretty. Are you really blonde?"

"Really. Well, not quite. It's gotten darker since I was little, so I have to touch it up."

Barbara Miller shrugs. "Tell me, Jennifer, do you have

friends in Los Angeles?" Mirror to mirror, a sharp glance. "No, I guess not. If you had friends, why would you be staying at the Y?"

"I've never been here before," new Jennifer defends. "I'm an orphan," she adds, as an orphan's theme, heart-melting, swells on imaginary strings.

"Lucky you. My old man drinks, and my mother's a witch."

Jennifer/Letty wonders, unkindly if fleetingly, if this latter trait might not be inheritable. There's something spooky about her new acquaintance, about her smug refusal of visual delight. "I'm sorry," Jennifer/Letty says.

"Don't be. As soon as I could leave, I left. That's that. How old are you?"

"I'm nineteen" says Jennifer, and Barbara Miller snorts her disapproval, whether of youth in general (she herself is agelessly plain) or at the particular congery of nineteen years, it is impossible to tell. A sniff follows the snort, and Barbara Miller's departure from the bathroom follows both. Our heroine, thank goodness, has no need, biological or psychological, to remain there longer. It is, as I picture it, a depressing place— the white–painted window transmitting no view and little light, the exposed pipes, though also painted white, pitted and deformed by cor-rosive age. Jennifer returns to her slightly less depressing hired room, sits at the small scarred desk and writes a letter not worth quoting home.

In fact, I wonder if her story is worth telling. It is my fault and prejudice to have imagined Letty/Jennifer a little dull. How could I not? The givens hemmed me in. A model (not an actress, not a poet, not a waitress, painter, seamstress, not an accountant, a doctor, a teacher, film editor, electrician, swimmer, gymnast)— a model, a decorative body devoid of discernible talent, whose ambition is for fame and romance, not for accomplishment, a young woman willing, given the givens, to live solely by her flesh,

and not so honestly as her seatmate whore, who was once presumably expert in the act of love and rewarded expenditure with
pleasure, a little anyway, but a model, selling the photographic
reversal of herself on film, goes to Hollywood.

It's boring, Susan. Or I at least am bored. I foresee no joy for
me imagining the producer she ensnares or who abuses her. If I
create a man of real talent and complexity to be antagonist or
lover or patron, he too will soon grow tired of our heroine. And I
would, if I were to proceed, serve up another of my ambivalent
endings, one of those inconclusive finishes that replicates the
chronic incompletion of real life.

I am too young, Susan, to write a happy ending; joy, to me, is
fleeting, and rightly so: how else but for its difference from the
usual churn and strum would we know it when it comes? Joy is
not the rainbow's end, but only a brief gift of sustaining levi-
tation along the way. There is only one ending fit or possible to
life in any case, once one eschews the fairy tale of immortality.
Letitia/Jennifer will be reduced to ashes soon enough— twice
immolated, perhaps, first in an imagined crematorium (ten
thousand wailing fans mourn on the steps), and once again when
this story ignites the fire and her tale ascends my chimney,
commingled with the morning smoke of neighbors burning news
and alder logs above a foggy coastal town, until a gust of wind off
the river drives the hovering ghosts up and beyond the guardian
mountains, away.

I can give my ingenue neither what she wants nor what I want,
and so perhaps it is kinder to lay the fire without delay. Only in
fiction can one create the character of one's children, only there
delineate their values. My flesh and blood children exhaust and
baffle me. The offspring of my precious solitude should— no, *must*
be people whom I love for cause, people who incite my admiration
or my empathy: the oddly brave, the eccentric dreamer, the

141

inarticulate survivor or too-verbal victim. My rightful heroines are generous women pinched by circumstance, my heroes lonely men compelled by principle, all motivated, finally, by love in one of its endless and inimitable disguises.

The novel shrinks to a story, the story to an excuse. My heart becomes a match I strike against the roughness of the world. The morning fire blazes in the grate. Farewell, my half-formed starlet. If you rise quickly enough from my chimney, you may yet catch the fading moon.

Susan, I hope you understand.

Yarn

"MR. FRED Borden, please."

"You got him."

"Mr. Borden, my name is Carrie, and I'm with the Rainbow Coalition."

"I don't want no dance lessons."

"I'm not selling anything, Mr. Borden. I'm calling— "

"So what's your pitch, honey?"

"I'm calling to ask you to support our candidate, the Reverend Jesse Jackson, in the presidential primary. I'd be happy to answer any questions…"

"I got a question for you. You white?"

"Mr. Borden, I don't see what…"

"You said you'd answer questions. You sound white. Are you?"

"Yes. I'm white."

"Then what the hell you doing trying to elect some nigger president for?"

Carrie hangs up and puts an X on the printout next to Borden, Fred. The campaign has no code for racist, so she draws a second X next to the first, for good measure. "Ignoramus." She says to the dead telephone what she would not to a living voter.

It's nine o'clock, quitting time. Any phone call made after 9 p.m. is more likely to lose than win a vote. Carrie accordion folds the precinct list, discards her Servomation cup and sweeps the last crumbs of her Oreos off the edge of the desk into her hand.

The phone bank organizers, a young woman and a young man, also white, interrupt their flirtation to bid Carrie good night. The boy wears jeans and a sweatshirt and has a student look. The girl's blonde hair is fashionably frizzed.

"I finished two lists and started a third," Carrie reports.

The girl's smile is full of practiced enthusiasm. "Great."

"A lot of people weren't home."

"At least we tried."

"Well, I'll just run along now."

"Can we put you down for Thursday night?"

"I'll come if I can," Carrie says.

"Great," they say, almost in unison. Before she's out of the office, they've returned to their teasing. Are they lovers yet? She thinks not. The girl's laugh is too giddy, the boy too cockily vulnerable, for the deed to have been done. Soon, perhaps tonight. Carrie met James at a May Day rally in— was it '36 or '37?

That's an argument for coming back Thursday night, to see if she can tell about the youngsters.

The bus drops her two blocks from her apartment house, and she walks briskly home. The neighborhood is ugly but not dangerous. For arc lamps and bus service she traded trees and quiet. It was, all things considered, a sensible exchange. James urged her to be prudent in her widowhood and she is, after her fashion, contriving to appear too old to provoke sexual assault and too fit to attract muggers in her gray coat and low-heeled shoes. After dark she never carries a purse but keeps her keys and wallet in the deep pockets of her coat. She is never afraid.

The lobby wallpaper in the Belmont Court is green on beige, an endless repetition, now faded, of someone's dream of elegance. A green tree-lined avenue leads to a green antebellum manor house. On a green bench in the green garden, two small green lovers sit, conversing deeply. From a distance, they appear courtly enough, but at close range, their faces are curiously grave, so that they resemble southern gentry less than two park bench radicals. It pleases Carrie to imagine their meeting is political, its subject not love, but shipment of cargo on the Underground Railway. The lobby is large enough for this meeting to take place some thirty times.

She has been in her apartment only long enough to take off her shoes, hang up her coat and put the kettle on when the door buzzer sounds the now-familiar summons. It's nearly ten o'clock, but Carrie doesn't mind the intrusion; her privacy is too vast to be seriously compromised by small invasions.

Would James have understood her small elation, opening the door, forgiven how her heart leaps up, seeing the wedge of henna hair and jumbled housecoat flowers, the blue plush rabbit ears and pink button eye of the one bedroom slipper the open door reveals? Carrie unhooks the chain to admit her visitor.

"I thought I heard you come in." Mrs. Olsen takes the tone of a worried mother, relieved at daughter's safe return. Her maternalism cloaks, almost excuses her eternal curiosity.

Carrie smiles. "I just got home."

"I suppose you took the bus again."

"Of course. It was right on time."

Mrs. Olsen hovers, her blue rabbit slippers bisected by the

threshold. "And I suppose you'll keep on riding the bus alone at night until something happens."

"Something always happens when I take the bus. Tonight a young boy with a mohawk haircut and one gold earring said, 'Hello, Mama.' I said, 'Good evening, son.' He sat down and we chatted."

"I suppose he asked you for money."

"He said his father was a gynecologist, with a successful practice in the West Hills. I should have asked him for a handout."

Mrs. Olsen will not relinquish her frown. "Maybe he has some kind of thing for older women. I've heard of that."

Carrie laughs. She is not sure it's entirely fair of her to make Mrs. Olsen make her laugh, but she enjoys it, and Mrs. Olsen seems not to mind. 'I was just about to make some tea. Would you like some?"

"I wouldn't want to keep you up. Maybe you'd rather be alone."

"What kind would you like? There's Earl Gray and jasmine and I think some chamomile."

Reassured, Mrs. Olsen comes in at last. "The kind that tastes like flowers, please," she says.

Carrie sets their teacups on the small dinette table. Mrs. Olsen breathes in the fragrant steam and emits an 'ah' of satisfaction. Before Carrie moved to the Belmont Court three months ago, Mrs. Olsen was strictly a Lipton drinker; she sips Carrie's herb teas as if they held some delicate and slightly wicked magic. Once she put her index finger in the cup and dabbed chrysanthemum tea behind her ears and in the wattled hollow of her throat, as if it were perfume.

Until the steam is gone, Mrs. Olsen huddles over her cup. Then, slowly, she begins to shift into her listening position, which is an inclined plane, head back, the heels of her bunny slippers planted in the rug, the whole posture supported by the vee of parted legs. Like most good gossips, Mrs. Olsen is an excellent listener. "So, where were you tonight?"

In her listening mode, Mrs. Olsen's eyes glisten, her expression is attentive and promises unconditional understanding. When Carrie is slow to answer, Mrs. Olsen says, "Unless you'd rather not say." Her inflection suggests that if Carrie chooses not to say, Mrs. Olsen will assume the worst, and Carrie wonders what, for Mrs. Olsen, the worst might be. Mrs. Olsen herself frequents bingo parlors and the dog track. Carrie answers truthfully. "I made eighty-nine telephone calls for Jesse Jackson."

"You wasted your time, then," Mrs. Olsen says. "This country isn't ready to elect a colored president."

"One might have said five years ago it would never elect an actor to the job."

"That's different."

"Especially a bad actor."

"He isn't so bad," Mrs. Olsen says. "Didn't you ever see the one where he's a football player and..."

"I saw it." She and James watched religiously when the local public TV station held a Ronald Reagan film festival. They were delighted to be appalled. America got, James said, what America deserved.

"Was your husband a Democrat, too?" Mrs. Olsen asks.

It's James she really wants to know about and always has been. All of her questions eventually lead back to James. Carrie's answers are always opaque.

James and Mrs. Olsen would never have gotten along. James disliked ignorance, complacency and prejudice; he detested hair-dye, housecoats and nosy neighbors, and he never was good at hiding his disdain, for people or ideas. Mrs. Olsen would have sensed it and disliked him back.

"He wasn't a Democrat," Carrie says. She doesn't say how

they both thought they were Communists, on meeting, back when it seemed the only sensible thing to be, before the Hitler-Stalin pact disabused them and the New Deal made democracy seem a quasi-hopeful proposition for a while, or that for years, they were partyless, espousers of causes, not candidates, or that most of their causes were too leftishly quixotic to have been successful. She does not tell Mrs. Olsen how graciously or with what resignation they accepted the gadfly role, becoming the necessary left, righteous but always faintly ridiculous, any more than she tells her that James was, when he died, her only friend.

Since James was not a Democrat, Mrs. Olsen assumes he was Republican. She fits the piece in place and nods. "My husband voted however I told him," she says. "He never liked to read and he thought the TV news was for falling asleep in front of. 'Elfie,' he'd say, 'you figure it out and let me know. I haven't got the time.' Of course, I never told him how to do the things he knew about. Bert was handy. He could fix anything that broke down. We sort of split things up."

Mrs. Olsen's eyes are unfocused, and Carrie knows that what she sees is Bert. Mrs. Olsen sniffs, sucking back sorrow, and Carrie finds it both hard and fascinating to look at her. Mrs. Olsen is almost comically unpretty, or makes herself that way with her too-bold attempts to outfox age— the henna rinses and the eyebrow pencil, the red red cheeks. Her nose is large, blanched white by face powder. Carrie wonders what her grief feels like, if it is similar to or wholly different from her own, if it ever simply numbs her, if she ever talks to Bert. Carrie suspects her own bereavement is both deeper and more exquisite, a nobler pain, and cordially detests herself for thinking so.

The old populist-elitist dilemma, James would have said, in one of his swift flights from emotion to analysis, but Carrie will not so willingly surrender her own ambivalence.

"He had a way with machines," Mrs. Olsen says, "and more tools than you ever saw."

Substitute ideas for machines, substitute books for tools. Mrs. Olsen is here and James is not. Mrs. Olsen is warm. Mrs. Olsen knows, not everything, but some things. Carrie says, "Sometimes I talk to James. Sometimes I even argue with him."

"Bert never argues," Mrs. Olsen says. "It wouldn't do him any good if he did." She laughs. "He's the one that's dead."

James is the one that's dead. Carrie wonders how it would feel to be James without Carrie. She wonders if she's alive, and breathes to prove it. She feels her pulse. The walls are white, these are her things— the green rug, the blue sofa, the dried flowers and the peacock feather. Two empty cups on the table. Her skin that feels cold.

She watched her grandmother unravel most of a sweater she'd been knitting once, just because she'd made a little mistake, dropped a stitch or something, way back. The yarn pulled out easy and it looked as if her grandmother enjoyed it, how unresistingly the yarn gave up being a sweater and became a twisted pile between her feet, crimped and a little frayed. Carrie feels like the yarn sometimes, curly and used, remembering the sweater.

After all her work was undone, her grandmother tackled the yarn, pulling it taut with one hand while she rolled it with the other into a ball that could be used again.

Carrie is trying to salvage the yarn. She is trying.

The apartment feels less foreign now than it did a month ago. The bookcases please her, reassure her, even though the books were the hardest thing to deal with, after James died. There were so many. Hers were old friends. His, in his absence, spoke for him. Twenty eight cartons she sold to Powell's and kept ten for herself. More than once, she's gone to Powell's to buy back a book she regretted selling. More than once, she's tried to read James' books, the history, philosophy and political theory. She wonders what Mrs. Olsen did with Bert's tools when he died.

She should go to bed, but the bed is empty. Maybe it was a mistake to keep their bed, maybe she should have sold it, too, and started fresh. It is an antique bed, white iron with knobs of blue glass shiny on its posts. It would have brought her a good price. Some nights she's clutched those iron bedposts, held them tight until sleep carried her away, and woke up clutching them still, her fingers stiff. Those nights, the holding-on nights, come less often now. More often now, she reads herself to sleep or thinks of James as she drowses down, not as someone she's lost, but as someone that she keeps.

Mrs. Olsen says it takes about a year and a half before one really starts to heal. Carrie is only five months convalescent. It gets better, Mrs. Olsen says. Carrie wants it to go fast.

"I'd start with three if I was you," Mrs. Olsen says. "They're hard to keep track of until you get the hang of it."

The cards are a dollar apiece, and Carrie feels wasteful, handing over her three folded bills. She and James never spent money frivolously; if there was extra, they bought books or sent small contributions to worthy causes. The woman to whom she gives her money has a Mamie Eisenhower haircut, straight bangs and lots of sidecurl, with teeth so unrealistically white and perfect in her lined face, Carrie knows they must be dentures.

The woman unfolds Carrie's dollars and puts them in a tray. "Take your pick," she says, without looking up.

Mrs. Olsen chooses her six cards carefully. "I'd play ten," she says, "except I can't afford it."

The hall is surprisingly full; at thirty long bare tables, only a few empty places remain. Mrs. Olsen spots two facing vacancies and hobbles toward them. She is wearing shoes, open-toed cracked patent leather sandals that hurt her feet. They sit on folding chairs. Mrs. Olsen holds up a card.

"See these little windows? When they call the number, you just pull the shade." With her thumbnail she tugs at a metal tab until black metal fills the recessed square and covers up the number underneath. "Center's free. When you cover up a whole row, horizontal, vertical or diagonal, you yell out 'BINGO' as fast as you can. Got that?"

Carrie nods. The woman next to Mrs. Olsen says, "Newcomer, huh," and Mrs. Olsen says, "Can you believe it." She arranges her cards in two rows of three, then pushes up "I'm going to get us some coffee before they start. It pays to keep alert." On her way to the coffee urn, Mrs. Olsen is waylaid by acquaintances and stops to visit.

In her absence, Carrie feels orphaned and out of place. She thought all Bingo games were held in church basements, but this is some kind of Republican club. Pictures of Republican presidents hang on the pale green walls— Ike statesmanly beside the flag, a mug shot of Richard Nixon with the sweat and stubble airbrushed out, the bland blank face of Gerald Ford— Carrie had almost forgotten about him— and a glossy movie studio publicity still of Ronald Reagan looking, as he always does to her, embalmed. She was grateful that James wanted cremation and spared her viewing cosmeticized remains.

One wall is given to the gilt-framed heroes of the GOP, Lincoln and Teddy Roosevelt, looking grizzled and historical. The people she sees around her are at least as old as she, the young adults of the Depression. This is a new class, the working class retired, gambling their pension checks, still hoping to strike it rich. James, you would not believe it. Unite. Arise.

"Here's cream and sugar if you want them," Mrs. Olsen says. She puts a paper cup and several little envelopes on the table. "So, you having fun?"

A round man in a green and orange plaid sport coat whistles through two fingers. His face is verdant from fluorescence passed through the green plastic of his visor.

"Look sharp," Mrs. Olsen says.

"First game is worth a hundred and fifty dollars," the visored man announces. The hall grows quiet as he spins the handle on a circular wire cage that looks like a gerbil's exercise machine filled up with Ping-Pong balls. He reaches into the cage, pulls out a yellow ball and reads, "B-Thirteen."

Carrie watches the players stoop to their cards. Mrs. Olsen's foot taps hers under the table. "Pay attention now, don't get behind."

"G-Forty-three," the caller calls.

"Beginner's luck," Mrs. Olsen says. "Too bad you had to split the pot." She lifts a forkful of lemon pie and puts it in her mouth. A froth of meringue clings to the corner of her mouth, where the blonde moustache hairs grow longest, and catches the light in its bubbles, glinting as she chews. Carrie is treating, since she won. Rose's Delicatessen is dim and at this hour full of dedicated eaters. Mrs. Olsen looks unnaturally confined at their two–person table, one shoulder pressed against the wall, the other over-reaching the chairback and intruding on the narrow rubber-runnered path the waitresses and busboys travel. Carrie fears she'll rub shoulders with a Bismarck or upend a chocolate eclair.

"Luck, anyway," she says. Subtract the price of three cards from her winnings and she's still seventy-two dollars ahead, pure windfall profit. Subtract two pies and teas from that—James would, but Carrie doesn't bother. Already she's mentally parcelling out the money between needs and luxuries.

152

"So," Mrs. Olsen says, "what are you going to do with the money?"

New underwear, maybe a little ribbon and lace on the panties. A bottle of Benedictine and Brandy for sipping from the silver liqueur glasses late at night— she can see herself, wearing her pink terrycloth bathrobe, a book in one hand, small smooth silver goblet in the other. The book is probably a novel. The drink is thickish but volatile, a little sweet and very warm. She can feel it distributing its warmth in her upper back and shoulders.

"Well?" Mrs. Olsen says.

"Well, I should probably see what's wrong with the television set and get it fixed and donate whatever's left over. Famine relief, I think, then Mondale-Ferraro, if there's any left over from that."

"When I win," Mrs. Olsen says, "I treat myself to something special. One time I won the blackout, six hundred dollars, and two days later I was on the bus to Reno." She pushes her empty pie plate to the side. "I stayed for three days. Played the slots. I'd win a little and put it back in. I wanted to see Wayne Newton, but I wanted to keep playing more. I felt like I was having a streak of luck, you know?"

"Did you win?" Carrie asks. She would like to ask about footwear, too. Picturing Mrs. Olsen in front of the slot machines, Carrie sees her wearing the blue rabbit slippers and Bert's old blue-gray cardigan, but knows this is probably wrong.

"The trip only cost me fifty three dollars out of pocket. I'd call that winning. More winning than your Jesse Jackson did."

"I didn't expect him to win," Carrie said. "That wasn't the point."

Mrs. Olsen resuscitates her crumpled tea bag with hot water from a small personal pot. "If it isn't the point, what is? Old Mondale and Ferraro aren't going to win either, you know."

"I think they have a chance."

"He's boring and she's married to a gangster," Mrs. Olsen says.

"That's media propaganda. Surely you don't believe everything you see on TV."

"Save your money," Mrs. Olsen says. "Buy yourself a new dress."

Carrie stares at the Events Calendar in Tuesday's paper. She would like to hear Helen Caldecott talk about the nuclear freeze, but she is tired of going everywhere alone, weary of seeking out intellectual stimulation when she has no partner and no hope of orgasm. This forced abstinence is almost worse than sleeping alone.

It was at the memorial service she realized that while she and James had many acquaintances, they had no friends. The service was well attended, the meeting hall was full of colleagues and fellow travellers, there were many handshakes but no hugs, abundant sympathy, but no comfort. The mailbox filled up with condolence cards, but no one called her on the phone.

For the privilege of living forty-seven years with her best friend, she pays dearly now, and blames James, who was so foresighted, for not foreseeing this.

"How come you know your way around so well?" Mrs. Olsen puffs to keep up with Carrie, crossing campus.

"James taught here for a while."

"I thought he was a bus driver."

"That was later. I worked here, too, in the library."

"Why would you give up a teaching job to drive a bus?"

"Bus drivers make more money," Carrie says. This may or may not be true, but it's definitely easier than explaining about the loyalty oath James wouldn't take. Mrs. Olsen accepts it.

Passing students gape at them, intruders in the preserve of

youth.   Mrs. Olsen is wearing her blue coat with the fake fur collar.   A filmy hot pink scarf half-hides her copper curls.   Her makeup is several times heavier for going out than it is for staying home.   Her eyelids, tonight, are shining midnight blue.   In the hall outside the auditorium, a couple she and James used to know hails Carrie.   He is a retired psychology professor.   His wife has never forgotten that she went to Bryn Mawr.   They are embarrassed to see Carrie, because they have forgotten her— the wife dies with the husband— and the woman can't take her eyes off Mrs. Olsen in her blue coat, her pink scarf and rhinestone earrings.   Carrie introduces her as 'my neighbor.'

"Where are you living?" the woman who went to Bryn Mawr asks, and her husband says, "We'll have to get together soon.   Give us a call."

Mrs. Olsen stares after them.   "Are those people friends of yours?"

"I've known them for a long time.   Why do you ask?"

"Because I couldn't tell," Mrs. Olsen says.

On the bus after the Caldecott lecture,   Mrs. Olsen is uncharacteristically quiet.   She stares out the window into the rain.

"What are you thinking about?" Carrie asks.

"The nightmare I'm going to have tonight.   What does she want to do that for anyway, scare people half to death?"

"If we don't face it, we can't stop it."

"We can't stop it," Mrs. Olsen says.   "So why face it?"

Carrie wends and weasels through the picketers until she's almost close enough to touch the young black man, close enough to hear that he chants with the others— South Africa's going to be free, South Africa's gotta be free— though his voice is soft, as if the words were prayers, not demands.   He is very tall and very thin, his face and hands the color of an almond's skin. Black hair writhes in curls down to his shoulders. Carrie has chosen him because his gravity, his implacable dignity remind her of James. Some of the others seem to be enjoying themselves too much; exuberance makes their motives suspect. Only this young man has the look of inviolate conviction.

Carrie touches his khaki sleeve. "Excuse me."

He looks down, around, before he sees her. Carrie did not expect to be flustered, but the young man's look is so intently questioning she feels her cheeks heat in a blush.

"Can I help you?"

"I hope so," Carrie says. "I want to get arrested."

He smiles. "Have you considered shoplifting?" When he sees her confusion, her blazing cheeks, he says, "I'm sorry. I couldn't resist."

"I understand. It *was* funny. Only I'm serious. What I mean to say is, I'm willing to be arrested."

The young man's only response is an intensification of his gaze.

"I'm not well known and I'm not black but I am willing. I thought you might be running low on volunteers. And my demographics are pretty good— I'm old and I'm a woman." Carrie knows she is blithering. All the arguments she used to convince herself she was a good candidate for arrest sound foolish and shallow spoken aloud.

The young man's silence outlasts her. She turns away.

"Wait a minute. Don't go."

Carrie turns back to him. "It's only because I care deeply. I should have said that first."

"I understand. But it's a serious step."

"I have nothing to lose. Less than you young folks. At my age, it's unlikely I'll be applying for another job."

"I've heard they're planning to lock the next batch up. No more Mr. Nice Guy. The cops are getting sick of us."

"I'm not afraid of jail."

The young man puts his hand on Carrie's shoulder; his voice is as light as his touch. "Give me your name and phone number. I'll talk to the committee."

Next Friday, James. I know it's not prudent, but it's right. Remember Trevor Huddlestone's book, back in the fifties? I think we sent them money. I know the government won't fall if we push the consul out of Portland, but it's something, isn't it? Not many things are wronger than apartheid.

Carrie sips her Benedictine and Brandy. The rim of the silver glass is magically, metallically cool. Catlike, she dips her tongue into the liquid and it burns. She has poured a second glass, out of courtesy and habit, and it sits on the coffee table, a little apart from her own.

And it's something to do. Can you understand how much I must do something? I'm less afraid of dying than of dissolving. Most days I'd be hard pressed to prove I'm not invisible. No one looks at old women, James, not even other old women. This is the worst job I've ever had.

I am complaining and I don't apologize. It's hard. It's goddamn bleak. And now I'm crying and my nose will get red but that's all right. I must have needed to cry. Do you know how hard it is to cry alone? I never understood before that it's an act requiring an audience.

I'm going to wear my brown skirt and my beige silk blouse and my sweater from Costa Rica, the white and brown one, to get arrested in. And when they tell me I'm under arrest, I'm going to say— in Portland I trespass on property rights because in South Africa, they trespass on human rights. Something like that. I haven't quite worked the words out yet, but I will.

Carrie refills her silver glass, sips and lets the liquid play on her tongue.

It's been a hard fall, James. We've lost some big ones. Greed has a new face these days, it's smiling and wholesome. Vast numbers of our countrymen have agreed to stop being embarrassed by their venality. The majority has decided: We shall live in a dream. It's no world for us. You can't talk back to a television script, and I can't dream their dream. That sleep's too deep, it's right next door to death. I struggle to stay awake, but the moral silence is seductive, James. That's why I need to get arrested.

Drink up, my love. It's really very good. I wish you'd drink it, even though if you did I'd probably have a heart attack or go mad. I dare you.

Do I have to drink it myself? To us, then. To the irony of us.

Friday comes brittle cold and sunny, a small miracle of weather in a city where winter means rain. The surge of Carrie's spirits, meeting the sun, feels like new growth, even though she knows spring is still long distant and this reprieve, only a trick of January. The air is so dry her hair spits sparks and crackles when she brushes it, and her apartment seems a sorry place to be, too dim and close on such a day.

Most mornings, she breakfasts slowly over the newspaper, but today from waking all her energy is spent towards escape. It's one of those days the world is careless of its secrets, willing to reveal its little beauties and anomalies. Carrie wants to wander and to watch. Later she will be arrested.

She dresses quickly but carefully, with pleasure. Her new brassiere and underpants, the first she's ever had that match, lie like a happy secret against her skin. She likes her body and her clothes today, she likes her face. Her step on the stairs is syncopated, a dignified gallop, and in the lobby she greets the nearest incarnation of the green park bench couple as if they were her co-conspirators.

Outside she trots toward the bus stop. The parking strips are frosty and tinfoil in the gutters glints like diamonds. The sharp wind makes her eyes cry griefless tears. In the absence of mirrors, her body feels young and strong.

Inside the bus hutch sits Mrs. Olsen, a squatty monument in blue. Escaping a bright red tam-o-shanter, the counterfeit copper of her hair frizzes electrically. Her green mesh shopping bag is empty. She looks up at Carrie and puffs a steamy greeting.

"Glorious day," Carrie says.

"Too cold." Mrs. Olsen inches over to make room for her on the bench. "Sit down."

"Thanks, but I feel like standing." Carrie stamps her feet. "It keeps me warm."

They sit together on the bus. "Where are you going?" Carrie asks.

"To pay my electric bill, and to the bank. Then I thought I'd check out the after-Christmas sales. You?"

"I'm going to be arrested."

Mrs. Olsen, who has heard everything, has not heard this. It takes her a moment to process the information. "Taxes?" she asks in a low voice.

"Politics."

"Jesus Lord, what have you done?"

"Nothing, yet. It's what I'm going to do."

And Mrs. Olsen, who has known Carrie for months, looks differently, and harder, frisking her pockets and her purse.

Carrie laughs. "No bombs. I'm going to perform a simple act of trespass at the South African consulate. The police will arrest me, then probably let me go."

Mrs. Olsen is somewhat reassured. "Did I see about that on the news?"

"Probably. There've been demonstrations twice a week for two months now."

"I thought it was all blacks."

"Not at all."

"What are you looking for trouble for?"

"I haven't felt so good for months."

"To each his own, I always say." Mrs. Olsen shakes her head. "Here I was thinking you looked so pretty you must've met a man."

"No man. A little vanity, maybe. I guess I wanted to look nice in case the news is there."

"Where and what time?" Mrs. Olsen wants to know. "I've got to see this."

Carrie gives her the address of the consul's office. "At noon," she says.

All morning she cherishes her impending celebrity, and the elation lasts— in Pioneer Courthouse Square, in the narrow aisles of her favorite bookstore, at Newberry's lunch counter where she orders a chocolate ice cream soda, despite the cold. From the flower vendor inside Newberry's door she buys a pink carnation and carries it with her, sometimes brushing the soft moist petals against her cheek, breathing its spring perfume, until she sees a bent woman in a black coat walking with a cane, a woman much older and sadder than she, scuttling slowly up the sidewalk with a three-beat gait. Carrie falls in beside her.

"Excuse me. This is for you." Carrie presses the flower into the woman's mittened hand and strides away, not looking back.

The civic clocks do not agree— one bank is fast, another slow, the jeweler's curbside clock face still shows daylight saving time, but at last it is something like the time, time to go, and Carrie turns toward the river, the consulate, toward the day's adventure. She makes herself walk slow, despite her rising pulse, breathes deeply, to steady nerves. Under her breath, she practices her state-ment—I have come—and the words emerge in little clouds of steam. She thinks of the young black man and his snaky hair, she wonders if the police will be polite when they arrest her, won-ders, with Mrs. Olsen, if there might be a man who is not James.

When Carrie rounds the corner on Third, the street is empty. There are no picketers, no signs, no songs. There are no televi-sion cameras and no police cars. A tweed-coated businessman steps out of the consul's office building and stops to pull on leather gloves before he turns into the street. The light changes and stops the passing cars. Fierce gusts of wind blow grit and litter up the sidewalk. In the pale January sunlight, the office buildings and pawn shops look flat and weightless, the plywood whimsies of a movie set.

For what seems like a long time there is no one to ask, no one but the ragged bum in his big stained coat and newspaper soles, whose shuffle turns to stagger when the wind gusts hard. Carrie looks away, willing him to pass quickly. He lurches up. "Lady, you got a cigarette?"

She makes herself look, at skin the color and texture of eroded brick, at irises bleeding into whites and whites cob-webbed red. "I'm sorry, I don't smoke."

"You got some money then? I want to buy a can of soup."

The wind carries his breath, a smell of deep decay. Today there is no change in her pockets. She hands the man a dollar bill.

"Thank you, ma'am. I appreciate it."

"Do you happen to know what time it is?" she asks.

161

"No ma'am. I pawned my watch."

"What day?"

"Afraid not, lady. One day's the same as the next to me. They all run together after a while."

"Yes, I know," Carrie says. "Get minestrone."

"What?"

"Your soup."

"Sure lady. Thanks again."

The next person to pass, a youngish woman, hides a watch under the knit wrist of her glove. "It's just a minute or two before noon."

"And it's Friday?"

"Friday the seventeenth."

Friday noon and the street is empty. Perhaps they changed the time, the day, the year. Perhaps even now, the demonstration is taking place in a different dimension, one parallel or perpendicular to her own. Perhaps, without knowing it, she has died. She crosses the street to enter the consul's office, but it sounds hollow and there are no crowds.

On the street, a woman in a bright blue coat with bright metallic hair walks toward her. Carrie had forgotten Mrs. Olsen.

"Where's the demonstration?"

"I don't know," Carrie says.

"At first I was afraid I missed it. You sure of the time?"

"I was." Carrie shivers in the bitter sunshine. Her voice is flat as Kansas. "Now I'm not sure of anything."

"Well, it's nothing to feel bad about. Who needs jail?"

"I don't understand it."

"Don't brood. It's too damn cold." Mrs. Olsen takes Carrie firmly by the arm. "I'll tell you what. We'll just go in this coffee shop and have a cup of tea."

Carrie allows herself to be led inside. They are the only

customers. They mount stools at the counter. Mrs. Olsen orders tea, then spots a newspaper abandoned at one of the tables and retrieves it. "You don't mind, do you? I haven't read my horoscope today. Say, maybe we should check yours, too. Maybe it'll tell us where the demonstration went."

While Mrs. Olsen searches the Living section for the horoscopes, Carrie finds the first section, sets right the order of the pages and scans the headlines. On the front page, below the fold, it says, "VANDERHOVEN RESIGNS. SOUTH AFRICAN CONSULATE TO CLOSE."

"Your birthday's July, right? It says here you'll locate lost or stolen article."

"It's over," Carrie says. "The consul quit. The demonstrations drove him to it."

"That's what you wanted, isn't it? That's good."

"It is good," Carrie says. "It's great. I'm delighted."

"It says I'm supposed to get a long distance phone call about money or love. Fat chance." Mrs. Olsen peers at Carrie around the paper's edge. "So how come you don't sound delighted?"

"I am. Of course I am. It's just that..."

"What?"

"It's hard to explain. I know it's foolish. James always said that ego is the enemy of political effectiveness, but I wanted it to be my victory, too. I *wanted* to get arrested."

"You were willing. That's what counts."

"Right. What's important is, it worked. The consul's gone." Carrie grips her teacup tightly in both hands. "I wish I were a better person."

"You're human," Mrs. Olsen says. "Big deal."

"Damn. I think I'm going to cry."

"I don't mind." Mrs. Olsen points to the proprietor, perched at the end of the counter with the crossword puzzle and a cup of coffee. "Neither does he."

Only a few tears come, just enough off the top to relieve pressure. She will not explode, not give up, not make a fool of herself in this quasi-public place. Tomorrow it will rain. She will get up and read the paper. In time she may learn to accept her unimportance.

"Say, you want to catch a movie? Only two dollars before five o'clock."

Carrie blows her nose on a coarse paper napkin. "Go ahead if you want to. I think I'll go home." Back to her burrow, the long dim drifting sleep. This is not real spring.

Mrs. Olsen pushes the newspaper aside and lays two dollars on the counter. "Me too. My feet are starting to bother me. Besides, there's always tomorrow." She slides off her stool, winces as her feet assume the burden of her weight. "Come on," she says to Carrie, and to the counterman calls, "Keep the change."

Carrie sits by the window, grateful for the bulk and warmth of Mrs. Olsen beside her. There is only so much space on the bus seat and no way to withdraw from contact. Mrs. Olsen's shoulder presses her, their thighs touch. Carrie sticks her cold hands in her armpits and feels drowsy. The passing of excitement leaves her drained of ambition. She desires nothing.

The winter sun is high overhead and casts no shadows. By its light, the people on the street look overexposed, washed clean of color. Their faces blur white with the motion of the bus. Carrie squints into the streets. Outside the library, on one of the cold stone benches always shaded by ornamental trees, she sees a slight man in a brown coat sitting meditatively, hands on his thin knees and head to one side; on the cold stone bench outside the library, Carrie sees an old man who looks just like James.